"We're not giving up n...

"Don't even think it."

"But are you...?"

"We are doing this." Her eyes had stars in them. "And we are taking home the prize."

"Brenna..." She smelled of flowers and fresh-cut grass. Travis really wanted to kiss her.

"Do it," she whispered, clearly reading his mind. "We need to do it. How can we pretend that we're headed for forever when you've never even put your lips on mine?"

Was she right? Did he really *need* to kiss her to make their fake relationship seem real? All he could think was that he'd never kissed her—and he *had* to kiss her.

He lowered his head a fraction closer and she surged up.

His mouth touched hers.

With a sigh, she let go of his shirtfront. Her hands slid up to clasp the back of his neck. "Travis..." She stroked his nape with her soft fingers as she whispered his name, kissing it onto his lips.

So good. So right. She tasted of honey, of ripe summer fruit—peaches and blackberries, watermelon. Cherries. She tasted of promises, sweet hopes and big dreams. She tasted of home.

Someone yelled, "Kiss her, cowboy!"

Neither Travis nor Brenna paid their hecklers any mind. The brims of their hats collided. His fell and then hers. Neither of them cared.

MONTANA MAVERICKS:
THE GREAT FAMILY ROUNDUP—
Real cowboys and real love in Rust Creek Falls!

Dear Reader,

Welcome back to Rust Creek Falls, Montana. This year, Travis Dalton, the fun-loving Dalton who always seemed allergic to settling down, has decided it's time to build his own house on the family ranch and step up to more responsibility, too. For that, he needs a nest egg.

And he knows just how to get what he needs. He's going to snare a spot on a brand-new cowboy reality show, *The Great Roundup*, which is filming this summer in Montana.

Brenna O'Reilly fell in love with Travis when she was six years old. It didn't work out. At first, when she was six and he was fourteen, he was too old for her. And later, well, Travis just wasn't the kind of guy looking to settle down. And you know what? Brenna's no settler either. She's always been the one inclined to leap before she looks—at least until lately, when she's started thinking a little settling wouldn't be bad. She wants to run her own business in the hometown she loves. But for that, she would need a nest egg.

And, as it turns out, Travis is just the man to help her with that. To succeed, they'll need to pretend to be something they're not: forever lovers. But, hey. No problem. Whatever it takes.

You know they'll get way more than they bargained for, right? Because if there did just happen to be a spark of attraction between them, pretending to be lovers who can't keep their hands off each other is no way to avoid starting a fire.

I love both Brenna and Travis, a pair of bold-hearted souls, both ready for anything. I hope you enjoy their wild and crazy journey to true love in *The Maverick Fakes a Bride!*

All my best,

Christine Rimmer

The Maverick Fakes a Bride!

Christine Rimmer

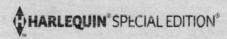

HARLEQUIN® SPECIAL EDITION®

Special thanks and acknowledgment are given to Christine Rimmer for her contribution to the Montana Mavericks: The Great Family Roundup continuity.

Recycling programs
for this product may
not exist in your area.

ISBN-13: 978-0-373-62356-3

The Maverick Fakes a Bride!

Copyright © 2017 by Harlequin Books S.A.

Printed in U.S.A.

www.Harlequin.com

Christine Rimmer came to her profession the long way around. She tried everything from acting to teaching to telephone sales. Now she's finally found work that suits her perfectly. She insists she never had a problem keeping a job—she was merely gaining "life experience" for her future as a novelist. Christine lives with her family in Oregon. Visit her at christinerimmer.com.

Visit the Author Profile page
at Harlequin.com for more titles.

For MSR,
always.

Chapter One

It was a warm day for March. And everyone in Bee's Beauty Parlor that afternoon had gathered at the wide front windows to watch as Travis Dalton rode his favorite bay gelding down Broomtail Road.

The guy was every cowgirl's fantasy in a snug Western shirt, butt-hugging jeans, Tony Lama Boots and a black hat. One of those film school graduates from the little theater in nearby Kalispell, a video camera stuck to his face, walked backward ahead of him, recording his every move. Travis talked and gestured broadly as he went.

"My, my, my." Bee smoothed her brassy blond hair, though it didn't need it. Even in a high wind, Bee's hair never moved. "Travis does have one fine seat on a horse."

There were soft, low sounds of agreement and appreciation from the women at the window—and then, out of nowhere, Travis tossed his hat in the air and flipped to a handstand right there on that horse in the middle of the street.

The women applauded. There was more than one outright cry of delight.

Only Brenna O'Reilly stood still and silent. She had her arms wrapped around her middle to keep from clapping, and she'd firmly tucked her lips between her teeth in order not to let out a single sound.

Because no way was Brenna sighing over Travis Dalton. Yes, he was one hot cowboy, with that almost-black hair and those dangerous blue eyes, that hard, lean body and that grin that could make a girl's lady parts spontaneously combust.

And it wasn't only his looks that worked for her. Sometimes an adventurous woman needed a hero on hand. Travis had come to her rescue more than once in her life.

But he'd always made a big deal about how he was too old for her—and okay, maybe he'd had a point, back when she was six and he was fourteen. But now that she'd reached the grown-up age of twenty-six, what did eight years even matter?

Never mind. Not going to happen, Brenna reminded herself for the ten thousandth time. And no matter what people in town might say, she was not and never had been in love with the man.

Right now, today, she was simply appreciating the view, which was spectacular.

Beside her, Dovey Jukes actually let out a moan and made a big show of fanning herself. "Is it just me, or is it *really* hot in here?"

"This is his, er, what did you call it now, Melba?" Bee asked old Melba Strickland, who'd come out from under the dryer to watch the local heartthrob ride by.

"It's his package," replied Melba.

Dovey snickered.

Bee let out her trademark smoke-and-whiskey laugh. "Not *that* kind of package." She gave Dovey a playful slap on the arm.

"It's reality television slang," Melba clarified. "Tessa told me all about it." Melba's granddaughter lived in Los Angeles now. Tessa Strickland Drake had a high-powered job in advertising and understood how things worked in the entertainment industry. "A package is an audition application and video."

"Audition for what?" one of the other girls asked.

"A brand-new reality show." Melba was in the know. "It's going to get made at a secret location right here in Montana this summer, and it will be called *The Great Roundup*. From what I heard, it's going to be like *Survivor*, but with cowboys—you know, roping and branding, bringing in the strays, everyone sharing their life stories around the campfire, sleeping out under the stars, answering challenge after challenge, trying not to get eliminated. The winner will earn himself a million-dollar prize."

Brenna, who'd never met a challenge she couldn't rise to, clutched the round thermal brush in her hand a little tighter and tried to ignore the tug of longing in her heart. After all, she'd been raised on the family ranch and could rope and ride with the best of them. She couldn't help but imagine herself on this new cowboy reality show.

True, lately, she'd been putting in some serious effort to quell her wild and crazy side, to settle down a little, you might say.

But a reality show? She could enjoy the excitement while accomplishing a valid goal of winning those big bucks. A few months ago, Bee had started dating a handsome sixtyish widower from Kalispell. Now that things had gotten serious, she'd been talking about selling the shop and retiring so she and her new man could travel. Brenna would love to step up as owner when Bee left.

But that would cost money she didn't have. If she won a million dollars on a reality show, however, she could buy the shop and still have plenty of money to spare.

And then again, no. Trying out for a reality show was a crazy idea, and Brenna was keeping a lid on her wild side, she truly was. *The Great Roundup* was not for her.

She asked wistfully, "You think Travis has a chance to be on the show?"

"Are you kidding?" Bee let out a teasing growl. "Those Hollywood people would be crazy not to choose him. And if the one doing the choosing is female, all that man has to do is give her a smile."

Every woman at that window enthusiastically agreed.

First week of May, a studio soundstage,
Los Angeles, California

Travis Dalton hooked his booted foot across his knee and relaxed in the interview chair.

It was happening. *Really* happening. His video had wowed them. And his application? He'd broken all the rules with it, just like that book he'd bought—*Be a Re-*

ality Star—had instructed. He'd used red ink, added lots of silly Western doodles and filled it chock-full of colorful stories of his life on the family ranch.

He'd knocked them clean out of their boots, if he did say so himself. And now here he was in Hollywood auditioning for *The Great Roundup*.

"Tell us about growing up on a ranch," said the casting director, whose name was Giselle. Giselle dressed like a fashion model. She had a way of making a guy feel like she could see inside his head. *Sharp*. That was the word for Giselle. Sharp—and interested. Her calculating eyes watched him so closely.

Which was fine. Good. He wanted her looking at him with interest. He wanted to make the cut, get on *The Great Roundup* and win himself a million bucks.

Travis gave a slow grin in the general direction of one of the cameras that recorded every move he made. "I grew up on my family's ranch in northwestern Montana." He was careful to include Giselle's question in his answer, in case they ended up using this interview in the show. Then they could cut Giselle's voice out and what he said would still make perfect sense. "My dad put me on a horse for the first time at the age of five. Sometimes it feels like I was born in the saddle."

Giselle and her assistant nodded their approval as he went on—about the horses he'd trained and the ones that had thrown him. About the local rodeos where he'd been bucked off more than one bad-tempered bull—and made it all the way to eight full seconds on a few. He thought it was going pretty well, that he was charming them, winning them over, showing them he wasn't shy, that an audience would love him.

"Can you take off your shirt for us, Travis?"

He'd assumed that would be coming. Rising, Travis unbuttoned and shrugged out of his shirt. At first, he kept it all business, no funny stuff. They needed to get a good look at the body that ranching had built and he kept in shape. He figured they wouldn't be disappointed.

But they wanted to see a little personality, too, so when Giselle instructed, "Turn around slowly," he held out his arms, bending his elbows and bringing them down, giving them the cowboy version of a bodybuilder's flex. As he turned, he grabbed his hat off the back of his chair and plunked it on his head, aiming his chin to the side, giving them a profile shot, and then going all the way with a slow grin and a wink over his shoulder.

The casting assistant, Roxanne, stifled a giggle as she grinned right back.

"Go ahead and sit back down," Giselle said. She wasn't flirty like Roxanne, but in her sharp-edged way she seemed happy with how the interview was shaking out.

Travis took off his hat again. He bent to get his shirt.

"Leave it," said Giselle.

He gave her a slight nod and no smile as he settled back into the chair. Because this was serious business. To him—and to her.

"Now we want to know about that hometown of yours." Giselle almost smiled then, though really it was more of a smirk. "We've been hearing some pretty crazy things about Rust Creek Falls."

Was he ready for that one? You bet he was. His town had been making news the past few years. First came the flood. He explained about the Fourth of July rains that wouldn't stop and all the ways the people of Rust Creek Falls had pulled together to come back from the worst disaster in a century. He spoke of rebuilding after the waters receded, of the national attention and the sudden influx of young women who had come to town to find themselves a cowboy.

When Giselle asked if any of those women had found *him*, he answered in a lazy drawl, "To tell you the truth, I met a lot of pretty women after the great flood." He put his right hand on his chest. "Each one of them holds a special place in my heart."

Roxanne had to stifle another giggle.

Giselle sent her a cool look. Roxanne's smile vanished as if it had never been. "Tell us more," said Giselle.

And he told them about a certain Fourth of July wedding almost two years ago now, a wedding in Rust Creek Falls Park. A local eccentric by the name of Homer Gilmore had spiked the wedding punch with his special recipe moonshine—purported to make people do things they would never do ordinarily.

"A few got in fights," he confessed, "present company included, I'm sorry to say." He made an effort to look appropriately embarrassed at his own behavior before adding, "And a whole bunch of folks got romantic—and that meant that *last* year, Rust Creek Falls had a serious baby boom. You might have heard of that. We called it the 'baby bonanza.' So now we have what amounts to a population explosion in our little town. Nobody's complaining, though. In Rust Creek Falls, love and family is what it's all about."

Travis explained that he wanted to join the cast of *The Great Roundup* for the thrill of it—and he also wanted to be the last cowboy standing. He had a fine life working the Dalton family ranch, but the million-dollar prize would build him his own house on the land he loved and put a little money in the bank, too.

"I'm not getting any younger," he admitted with a smile he hoped came across as both sexy *and* modest. "One of these days, I might even want to find the right girl and settle down."

Giselle, who had excellent posture in the first place, seemed to sit up even straighter, like a prize hunting dog catching a scent. "The right girl? Interesting." She glanced at Roxanne, who bobbed her head in an eager nod. "Is there anyone special you've got your eye on?"

There was no one, and there probably wouldn't be anytime soon. But he got Giselle's message loud and clear. For some reason, the casting director would prefer that he had a sweetheart.

And what Giselle preferred, Travis Dalton was bound and determined to deliver. "Is there a special woman in my life? Well, she's a…very private person."

"That would be yes, then. You're exclusive with someone?"

Damn. Message received, loud and clear. He wasn't getting out of this without confessing—or lying through his teeth. And since he intended to get on the show, he knew what his choice had to be.

"I don't want to speak out of hand, but yeah. There is a special someone in my life now. We…haven't been together long, but…" He let out a low whistle and pasted on an expression that he hoped would pass for completely smitten. "Oh, yeah. *Special* would be the word for her."

"Is this special someone a hometown girl?" Giselle's eyes twinkled in a way that was simultaneously aggressive, gleeful and calculating.

"She's from Rust Creek Falls, yes. And she's amazing." *Whoever the hell she is.* "It's the greatest thing in the world, to know someone your whole life and then suddenly to realize there's a lot more going on between the two of you than you've ever admitted before." Whoa. He probably ought to be ashamed of himself. His mama had brought him up right, taught him not to tell lies. But who did this little white lie hurt, anyway? Not a soul. And to get on *The Great Roundup*, Travis Dalton would tell Giselle whatever she needed to hear.

"What's her name?" asked Giselle. It was the next logical question, damn it. He should have known it was coming.

He put on his best killer smile—and lied some more. "Sorry, I can't tell you her name. You know small towns." Giselle frowned. She might be sharp as a barbwire fence, but he would bet his Collin Traub dress saddle that she'd never been within a hundred miles of a town like Rust Creek Falls. "We're keeping what we have together just between the two of us, my girl and me. It's a special time in our relationship, and we don't want the whole town butting into our private business." *A special time.* Damned if he didn't sound downright sensitive—for a bald-faced liar. But would the casting director buy it?

Giselle didn't seem all that thrilled with his unwillingness to out his nonexistent girlfriend, but at least she let it go. A few minutes later, she gave the cameraman a break. Then she chatted with Travis off the record for a couple of minutes more. She said she'd heard he was staying at the Malibu house of LA power player Carson Drake, whose wife, Tessa Strickland Drake, had deep Montana roots. Travis explained that he'd known Tessa all his life. She'd grown up in Bozeman, but she spent most of her childhood summers staying at her grandmother's boardinghouse in Rust Creek Falls.

After the chitchat, Giselle asked him to have a seat outside. He put on his shirt and grabbed a chair in the waiting area next to a watercooler and vending machine. For the next few hours, he watched potential contestants come and go.

It was past six when they called him back in to tell him that he wouldn't be returning to Malibu that night—or anytime soon, as it turned out. Real Deal Entertainment would put him up in a hotel room instead.

Travis lived in that hotel room for two weeks at Real Deal's beck and call. He took full advantage of room service, and he worked out in the hotel fitness center to pass the time while he got his background checked and his blood drawn. He even got interviewed by a shrink, who asked a lot of way-too-personal questions. There were also a series of follow-up meetings with casting people and producers. At the two-week mark, in a Century City office tower, he got a little quality time with a bunch of network suits.

That evening, absolutely certain he'd made the show, he raided the minibar in his room and raised a toast to his success.

Hot damn, he'd done it! He was going to be a contestant on *The Great Roundup*. He would have his shot at a cool million bucks.

And he would win, too. Damned if he wouldn't. He would build his own house on the family ranch and get more say in the day-to-day running of the place. His older brother, Anderson, made most of the decisions now. But if Travis had some hard cash to invest, his big brother would take him more seriously. Travis would step up as a real partner in running the ranch.

Being the good-time cowboy of the family had been fun. But there comes a point when every man has to figure out what to do with his life. Travis had reached that point. And *The Great Roundup* was going to take him where he needed to go.

The next morning, a car arrived to deliver him to the studio, where he sat in another waiting area outside a different soundstage with pretty much the same group of potential contestants he'd sat with two weeks before. One by one, they were called through the door. They all emerged smiling to be swiftly led away by their drivers.

When Travis's turn came, he walked onto the sound-stage to find Giselle and Roxanne and a couple producers waiting at a long table. The camera was rolling. Except for that meeting in the office tower with the suits and a session involving lawyers with papers to sign, a camera had been pointed at him every time they talked to him.

Giselle said, "Have a seat, Travis." He took the lone chair facing the others at the table. "We have some great news for you."

He knew it—he was in! He did a mental fist pump.

But then Giselle said, "You've made the cut for the final audition."

What the hell? *Another* audition?

"You'll love this, Travis." Giselle watched him expectantly as she announced, "The final audition will be in Rust Creek Falls."

Wait. What?

She went on, "As it happens, your hometown is not

far from the supersecret location where *The Great Roundup* will be filmed. And since your first audition, we have been busy…"

Dirk Henley, one of the producers, chimed in, "We've been in touch with the mayor and the town council."

"Of Rust Creek Falls?" Travis asked, feeling dazed. He was still trying to deal with the fact that there was more auditioning to get through. He couldn't believe she'd just said the audition would be happening in his hometown.

"Of course, of Rust Creek Falls." Giselle actually smiled, a smile that tried to be indulgent but was much too full of sharp white teeth to be anything but scary.

Dirk took over again. "Mayor Traub and the other council members are excited to welcome Real Deal Entertainment to their charming little Montana town."

Travis valiantly remained positive. Okay, he hadn't made the final cut, but he was still in the running and that was what mattered.

As for the final audition happening at home, well, now that he'd had a second or two to deal with that information, he supposed he wasn't all that surprised.

For a show like *The Great Roundup*, his hometown was a location scout's dream come true. And the mayor and the council would say yes to the idea in a New York minute. The movers and shakers of Rust Creek Falls had gotten pretty ambitious in the last few years. They were always open to anything that might bring attention, money and/or jobs to town. Real Deal Entertainment should be good for at least the first two.

Dirk said, "We'll be sending Giselle, Roxanne, a camera crew *and* a few production people along with you for a last on-camera group audition."

Giselle showed more teeth. "We're going to put you and your fellow finalists in your own milieu, you might say."

Dirk nodded his approval. "And that milieu is a very atmospheric cowboy bar with which I'm sure you are familiar."

There was only one bar inside the Rust Creek Falls town limits. Travis named it. "The Ace."

"That's right!" Dirk beamed. "The Ace in the Hole, which we love."

What did that even mean? They loved the name? Must be it. No Hollywood type would actually *love* the Ace. It was a down-home, no-frills kind of place.

Dirk was still talking. "We'll be taking over 'the Ace'—" he actually air quoted it "—for a night of rollicking country fun. You know, burgers and brews and a country-western band. We want to see you get loose, kick over the traces, party in a purely cowboy sort of way. It will be fabulous. You're going to have a great time." He nodded at the other producer, who nodded right back. "I'm sure we'll get footage we can use on the show."

And then Giselle piped up with, "And, Travis…" Her voice was much too casual, much too smooth. "We want you to bring your fiancée along to the audition. We love what you've told us about her, and we can't wait to meet her."

Chapter Two

Fiancée?

Travis's heart bounced upward into his throat. He tried not to choke and put all he had into keeping his game face on.

But…

Fiancée? When did his imaginary girlfriend become a fiancée?

He'd never in his life had a fiancée. He hadn't even been with a woman in almost a year.

Yeah, all right. He had a rep as a ladies' man and he knew how to play that rep, but all that, with the women and the wild nights? It had gotten really old over time. And then there was what had happened last summer. After that, he'd realized he needed to grow the hell up. He'd sworn off women for a while.

Damn. This was bad. Much worse than finding out

there was still another audition to get through. How had he not seen this coming?

Apparently, they'd decided they needed a little romance on the show, a young couple in love and engaged to be married—and he'd let Giselle get the idea that he could give them that. He'd thought he was playing the game, but he'd only played himself.

He tried to put on the brakes a little. "Uh, Giselle. We're not exactly engaged yet."

"But you will be." It was a command. And before he could figure out what to say next, Giselle stood. "So, we're set then. You'll be taken back to the hotel for tonight. Pack up. Your plane leaves first thing tomorrow."

Travis had come this far, and he wasn't about to give up now. Somehow, he needed to find himself a temporary fiancée. She had to be outgoing and pretty, someone who could ride a horse, build a campfire and handle a rifle, someone he could trust, someone he wouldn't mind pretending to be in love with.

And she had to be someone from town.

It was impossible. He knew that. But damn it, he was not giving up. Somehow, he had to find a way to give Giselle and the others what they wanted.

Real Deal Entertainment had a van waiting at the airport in Kalispell. The company had also sent along a production assistant, Gerry, to ride herd on the talent. Gerry made sure everyone and their luggage got on board the van and then drove them to Maverick Manor, a resort a few miles outside the Rust Creek Falls town limits.

Gerry herded them to the front desk. As he passed out the key cards, he announced that he was heading

back to the airport to pick up the next group of finalists. They were to rest up and order room service. The
producers and casting director would be calling everyone together first thing tomorrow right here in the
main lobby.

Travis grabbed Gerry's arm before he could get
away. "I need to go into town." *And rustle up a fiancée.*

Gerry frowned—but then he nodded. "Right. You're
Dalton, the local guy. You can get your own ride?"

"Yeah." A ride was the least of his problems.

Gerry regarded him, narrow eyed. Travis understood. As potential talent, the production company
wanted him within reach at all times. He wouldn't be
free again until he was either culled from the final cast
list—or the show had finished shooting, whichever happened first.

Travis was determined not to be culled. "I'm supposed to bring my fiancée to the audition tomorrow
night. I really need to talk to her about that." *As soon
as I can find her.*

Gerry, who was about five foot six and weighed
maybe 110 soaking wet, glared up at him. "Got it. Don't
mess me up, man."

"No way. I *want* this job."

"Remember your confidentiality agreement. Nothing about the production or your possible part in it gets
shared."

"I remember."

"Be in your room by seven tonight. I'll be checking."

"And I'll be there."

Gerry headed for the airport, and Travis called the
ranch. His mother, Mary, answered the phone. "Honey,
I am on my way," she said.

He was waiting at the front entrance of the Manor when she pulled up in the battered pickup she'd been driving for as long as he could remember. She jumped out and grabbed him in a bear hug. "Two weeks in Hollywood hasn't done you any damage that I can see." She stepped back and clapped him on the arms. "Get in. Let's go."

She talked nonstop all the way back to the ranch—mostly about his father's brother, Phil, who had recently moved to town from Hardin, Montana. Phil Dalton had wanted a new start after the loss of Travis's aunt Diana. And Uncle Phil hadn't made the move alone. His and Diana's five grown sons had packed up and come with him.

At the ranch, Travis's mom insisted he come inside for a piece of her famous apple pie and some coffee.

"I don't have that long, Mom."

"Sit down," Mary commanded. "It's not gonna kill you to enjoy a slice of my pie."

So he had some pie and coffee. He saw his brother Anderson, briefly. His dad, Ben, was still at work at his law office in town.

Zach, one of Uncle Phil's boys, came in, too. "That pie looks really good, Aunt Mary."

Mary laughed. "Sit down and I'll cut you a nice big piece."

Zach poured himself some coffee and took the chair across from Travis. In his late twenties, Zach was a good-looking guy. He asked Travis, "So how's it going with that reality show you're gonna be on?"

Travis kept it vague. "We'll see. I haven't made the final cut yet."

Zach shook his head. "Well, good luck. I don't get

the appeal of all that glitzy Hollywood stuff. I'm more interested in settling down, you know? Since we lost Mom…" His voice trailed off, and his blue eyes were mournful.

"Oh, hon." Trav's mom patted Zach gently on the back. She returned to the stove and added over her shoulder, "It's a tough time, I know."

"So sorry about Aunt Diana," Travis said quietly.

Zach nodded. "Thank you both—and like I was sayin', losing Mom has reminded me of what really matters, made me see it's about time I found the right woman and started my family."

Travis ate another bite of his mother's excellent pie and then couldn't resist playing devil's advocate on the subject of settling down. "I can't even begin to understand how tough it's been for you and your dad and the other boys. But come on, Zach. You're not even thirty. What's the big hurry to go tying the knot?"

Zach sipped his coffee. "You would say that. From where I'm sitting, Travis, you're a little behind the curve. All your brothers and sisters—and more than a few cousins—are married and having babies. A wife and kids, that's what life's all about."

"I'll say it again. There's no rush." Well, okay. For him there kind of was. He needed a fiancée, yesterday or sooner. But a wife? Not anytime soon.

Travis's mother spoke up from her spot at the stove. "Don't listen to him, Zach. If a wife is what you're looking for, you've come to the right place. There are plenty of pretty, smart, marriageable young women in Rust Creek Falls. Marriage is in the air around here."

Travis grunted. "Or it could be something in the water. Whatever it is, Mom's right. Marriage is nothing short of contagious in this town. Everybody seems to be coming down with it."

Zach forked up his last bite of pie. "Sounds like Rust Creek Falls is exactly the place that I want to be."

It was almost three in the afternoon when Travis climbed in his Ford F-150 crew cab and went to town.

He drove up and down the streets of Rust Creek Falls with the windows down, waving and calling greetings to people he knew, racking his brain for a likely candidate to play the love of his life on *The Great Roundup*.

Driving and waving were getting him nowhere. He decided he'd stop in at Daisy's Donut Shop—just step inside and see if his future fake fiancée might be waiting there, having herself a maple bar and coffee.

He found a spot at the curb in front of Buffalo Bill's Wings To Go, which was right next door to Daisy's. As he walked past, he stuck his head in Wings To Go. No prospects there. He went on to the donut shop, but when he peered in the window, he saw only five senior citizens and a young mother with two little ones under five.

Not a potential fiancée in sight.

Trying really hard not to get discouraged, he started to turn back for his truck. But then the door to the adjacent shop opened.

Callie Crawford, a nurse at the local clinic, came out of the beauty parlor. "Thanks, Brenna," Callie called over her shoulder before letting the door shut. She spotted Travis. "Hey, Travis! I heard about you and that reality show. Exciting stuff."

"Good to see you, Callie." He tipped his hat to her. "Final audition is tomorrow night."

"At the Ace, so I heard. We're all rooting for you."

He thanked her and asked her to say hi to her husband, Nate, for him. With a nod and a smile, Callie got in her SUV and drove off.

And that was it. That was when it happened. He watched Callie drive off down the street when it came to him.

Brenna. Brenna O'Reilly.

Good-looking, smart as a whip and raised on a ranch. She'd taken some ribbons barrel racing during the three or four summers she worked the local rodeo circuit. She was bold, too. Stood up for herself and didn't take any guff.

But he'd always considered himself too old for her. Plus, he kind of thought of himself as a guy who looked out for her. He would never make a move on her.

However, this wouldn't be a move.

Uh-uh. This would be…an opportunity.

If she was interested and if it was something she could actually handle.

Brenna.

Did he have any other prospects for this?

Hell, no.

He had less than three hours to find someone. At this point, it was pretty much Brenna or bust.

By then, he was already opening the door to the beauty shop. A bell tinkled overhead as he went in.

Brenna was standing right there, behind the reception counter with the cash register on it, facing the door. She looked kind of surprised at the sight of him.

Before either of them could say anything, the owner, Bee, spotted him. "Travis Dalton!" She waved at him with the giant blow-dryer in her left hand. "What do you know? It's our local celebrity."

Every woman in the shop turned to stare at him. He took off his hat and put on his best smile. "Not a celebrity *yet*, Bee. Ladies, how you doing?"

A chorus of greetings followed. He nodded and kept right on smiling.

Bee asked, "What can we do for you, darlin'?"

He thought fast. "The big final audition's tomorrow night."

"So we heard."

"Figured I could maybe use a haircut—just a trim." He hooked his hat on the rack by the door. "So, Brenna, you available?"

Brenna's blue eyes met his. "You're in luck. I've got an hour before my next appointment." She came out from behind the counter, looking smart and sassy in snug jeans, ankle boots and a silky red shirt. Red worked for her. Matched her hair, which used to be a riot of springy curls way back when. Now she wore it straight and smooth, a waterfall of fire to just below her shoulders.

She waited until he'd hung up his denim jacket next to his hat then led him to her station. "Have a seat."

He dropped into the padded swivel chair and faced his own image in the mirror.

Brenna put her hands on his shoulders and leaned in. He got a whiff of her perfume. Nice. She caught his eye in the mirror and then ran her fingers up into his hair, her touch light, professional. "This looks pretty good."

It should. He'd paid a lot to a Hollywood stylist right before that first audition two weeks ago. "I was thinking just a trim."

She stood back, nodding, a dimple tucking into her

velvety cheek as she smiled. "Well, all right. You want a shampoo first?"

What he wanted was to talk to her alone. He cast a glance to either side and lowered his voice. "Say, Brenna…"

She knew instantly that he was up to something. He could tell by the slight narrowing of her eyes and the way the bow of her upper lip flattened just a little. And then she leaned in again and whispered, "What's going on?"

He went for it. "I was wondering if I could talk to you in private."

Her sleek red-brown eyebrows drew together. "Right now?"

"Yeah."

"Where?"

He cast a quick glance around and spotted the hallway that led to the parking area in back. "Outside?"

She folded her arms across her chest and tipped her head to the side. "Sure. Go on out back. I'll be right there."

"Thanks." He got right up and headed for the back door, not even pausing to collect his jacket and hat. It wasn't that cold out, and he could get them later.

"What's going on?" Bee asked as he strode past her station.

Brenna answered for him. "Travis and I need to talk."

Somebody giggled.

Somebody else said, "Oh, I'll just bet you do."

Travis kept walking. It was okay with him if everyone at the beauty shop assumed he was finally making a move on Brenna—because he was.

Just not exactly in the way that they thought.

Outside, he looked for a secluded spot and settled on the three-walled nook where Bee stored her Dumpster. It didn't smell too bad, and the walls would give them privacy.

He heard the back door open again and stuck his head out to watch Brenna emerge. "Psst."

She spotted him and laughed. "Travis, what *is* this?"

He waved her forward. "Come on. We don't have all day."

For that he got an eye roll, but she did hustle on over to the enclosure. "All right, I'm here. Now what is it?"

He had no idea where to even start. "I…I have a proposal."

Her eyelashes swept down and then back up again. "Excuse me?"

"This… What I'm about to say. I need your solemn word you won't tell a soul about any of it, or I'll get sued for breach of contract. Understand?"

"Not really." She chewed on her lower lip for a moment. "But okay. I'm game. I won't tell a soul. You have my sworn word on that." She hooked her pinkie at him. He gave it a blank look. "Pinkie promise, Trav. You know that is the most solemn of promises and can never be broken."

"What are we, twelve?"

She made a little snorting sound. "Oh, come on."

He gave in and hooked his pinkie with hers. "Satisfied?"

"*Are you?* Because that is the question." She laughed, a sweet, musical sound, and tightened her pinkie against his briefly before letting go.

"As long as you promise me."

"Travis. I promise. I will tell no one, no matter what happens. Now what is going on?"

"How'd you like to be on *The Great Roundup*?"

She wrinkled her nose at him. "What? How? You're making no sense."

"Just listen, okay? Just give me a chance. I...well, I really thought I had it, you know? I thought I was on the show. But it turns out they want a young couple. A young, *engaged* couple. And the casting director sort of asked me if there was anyone special back home and I sort of said yes. And then, all of a sudden, they tell me there's one final audition, that it will be at the Ace and I should bring my fiancée."

Brenna's eyes were wide as dinner plates. "You told them you were *engaged*?"

"No, I didn't *tell* them that. They assumed it. And now I need a fake fiancée, okay? I need someone who doesn't mind putting herself out there, if you know what I mean. Someone who's not going to be afraid to speak up and hold her head high when the cameras are rolling. Someone good-looking who's familiar with ranch work, who can ride a horse and handle a rifle."

Brenna grinned then. "So you think I'm good-looking, huh?"

"Brenna, you're gorgeous."

"Travis." She looked like she was having a really good time. "Say that again."

Why not? It was only the truth. "Brenna, you are superfine."

And she threw back her red head and let her laughter chime out. He stood there and watched her and thought how he'd known her since she was knee-high to a gnat. And that she was perfect, just what he needed to make

Giselle happy—and earn him his spot on *The Great Roundup*.

But then she stopped laughing. She lowered her head and she regarded him steadily. "So say that it worked— say I go to the Ace with you tomorrow night and we convince them that we're together, that we're going to get married. Then what?"

"Then you belong to them for the next eight to ten weeks. First while they run checks on you and make sure you're healthy, mentally stable and have never murdered anyone or anything."

"You're not serious."

"As a rattler on a hot rock. And as soon as all that's over, we start filming. That's happening at some so far undisclosed Montana location. We're there until they're through filming."

"But what if I get eliminated? *Then* can I come home?"

He shook his head. "Everyone stays. So they can bring you back on camera if they want to, and also because if you come home early, everyone who knows you will know you've been eliminated. They want to keep the suspense going as to who the big winner is until the final show airs. Also, when the filming's over and you come home, you and I would still be pretending to be engaged."

"Until?"

"The episodes where we've each been eliminated have aired— or the final episode, where one of us wins. The show airs once a week, August through December. Bottom line, you could be my fake fiancée straight through till Christmas."

She leaned against the wall next to the Dumpster

and wrapped her arms around herself. "Wow. I...don't know what to say."

He resisted the burning need to promise her that they would win and that she was going to love it. "It's a lot to take in, I know."

She slanted him a glance. "I'd have to check with Bee, see if she'd hold my station for two months."

He refused to consider that Bee might say anything but yes. "I get that, sure."

"And then there's the money. I heard the winner gets a million dollars."

"Actually, once you get on the show, there's a graduated fee scale. The million is the top prize, but everybody gets something."

She leaned toward him a little, definitely interested. "Graduated how?"

"The first one eliminated gets twenty-five hundred. The longer you stay in the game, the more you get. For instance, if you last through the sixth show, you get ten thousand. And if you're the last to go before the winner, you get a hundred K."

She actually chuckled. "Good to know. So, Travis, if we're in this together, I say we split everything fifty-fifty."

He'd figured on giving her something, but he'd been kind of hoping she'd settle for much less. After all, he had big plans for his new house, for the ranch. He cleared his throat. "Would you take twenty percent?"

"Travis," she chided.

"Thirty?" he asked hopefully.

"Look at it this way. If they like me and want me on the show, you double your chances to win. Not to mention, the longer we both stay on, the more we both make." She spoke way too patiently. He found himself wistfully recalling the little girl she'd once been, the little girl who'd considered him her own personal hero and would have done anything he asked her to do, instantly, without question. Where had that little girl gone?

"True, but I'm your ticket in," he reminded her. "I'm the one who worked my ass off getting this far, you know?"

"I see that. And I admire that. I sincerely do. But without me, you won't make the cast."

She was probably right. He argued, anyway. "I'm not sure of that."

Brenna was silent, leaning there against the wall, her head tipped down. The seconds ticked by. He waited, trying to look easy and unconcerned, playing it like he didn't have a care in the world. Too bad that inside he was a nervous wreck.

Finally, she looked up and spoke again. "I'm trying not to be so impulsive in my life, to settle down a little, you know what I mean?"

Their eyes met and they gazed at each other for a long count of ten. "Bren. I know exactly what you mean."

She gave a chuckle, sweet and low. "I kind of thought that you might. The thing is, playing your fake fiancée on a reality show is not exactly what I would call settling down. And what are the odds against us, anyway? How many will end up competing with us?"

"I think there are twenty-two contestants total, so it's you and me and twenty others."

"Meaning that however we split the money, odds are someone else will take home the big prize."

He pushed off the wall, took her by the shoulders and looked deeply into those ocean-blue eyes. "First rule.

Never, *ever* say we might not win. We *will* win. Half the battle is the mental game. Defeat is not an option. Winning is the only acceptable outcome."

She got it, she really did. He could feel it in the sudden straightening of her shoulders beneath his hands, see it in the bright gleam that lit those wide eyes. "Yeah. You're right. We *will* win."

"That's it. Hold that thought." He let go of her shoulders but held her gaze.

She said, "We really would be increasing our chances, the two of us together. Together, we can work out strategies, you know? We can plan how to handle whatever they throw at us."

"Exactly. We would have each other's backs. So what do you say, Bren?"

"I still want half the money." A gust of wind slipped into the three-sided enclosure and stirred her hair, blowing a few fiery strands across her mouth.

He smoothed them out of the way, guiding them behind her ear, thinking how soft her pale skin was and marveling at how she'd grown up to be downright hot. It was a good thing he'd always promised himself he'd never make a move on her. Add that promise to the fact that he'd sworn off women and he should be able to keep from getting any romantic ideas about her.

"Travis?" She searched his face. "Did you hear what I just said?"

"I heard." He ordered his mind off her inconvenient hotness and set it on coming up with more reasons she should take less than half the prize.

Unfortunately, he couldn't think of a single one.

So all right, then. His new house and his investment in the ranch would be smaller. But his chances of winning had just doubled—*more* than doubled. Because Brenna was a fighter, and together they *would* go all the way to the win.

"Fair enough, Bren. Fifty-fifty, you and me." He held up his hand.

She slapped a high five on it. "I'll be right back."

He caught her before she could get away. "There's more we need to talk about."

"Not until I get the okay from Bee, we don't." She glanced down at his fingers wrapped around her upper arm.

He let go. "What will you say to her?"

"That I might have a chance on *The Great Roundup*, but to try for it, I need to know that she'll let me have my booth back on August 1."

"Good. That's good. Don't mention the engagement yet. We still need to decide how to handle that."

She let out another sweet, happy laugh—and then mimed locking her mouth and tossing away the key. "My lips are sealed," she whispered, then whirled on her heel and headed for the back door.

Five endless minutes later, she returned.

"Well?" he asked, his heart pounding a worried rhythm beneath his ribs.

Her smile burst wide open. "Bee wished us luck."

"And?"

"Yes, she'll hold my booth for me."

He almost grabbed her and hugged her, but caught himself in time. "Excellent."

"Yeah—and is there some reason we need to hang around out here? Let's go in. I'll give you that trim you pretended you needed."

He heard a scratching sound, boots crunching gravel. "What's that?"

He signaled for silence and stuck his head out of the enclosure in time to see the back of crazy old Homer Gilmore as he scuttled away across the parking lot toward the community center on Main, the next street over.

Brenna stuck her head out, too. "It's just Homer."

They retreated together back into the enclosure. He asked, "You think he heard us?"

She was completely unconcerned. "Even if he did, Homer's not going to say anything."

"And you know this how?"

"He's a little odd, but he minds his own business."

"A *little* odd? He's the one who spiked the punch with moonshine at Braden and Jennifer's wedding two years ago."

"So?" The wind stirred her hair again. She combed it back off her forehead with her fingers. "He never gossips or carries tales. To tell you the truth, I trust him."

"Because…?"

"It's just, well, I don't know. I have this feeling that he looks out for me, like a guardian angel or a fairy godmother."

Travis couldn't help scoffing, "One who just happens to be a peculiar old homeless man."

"He's not homeless. People just assume he is. He's got a shack on Falls Mountain he stays in."

"Who told you that?"

"He did. And he's not going to say anything. I guarantee it. Now, let's go in and—"

Travis put up a hand. "Just a minute. A couple more things. Starting tomorrow night, we're madly in love.

You'll need to convince a bunch of LA TV people that I'm the only guy for you."

"Well, that's a lot to ask," she teased. "But I'll do my best."

"You'll need to make everyone in town believe it, too—including your family. They all have to think we're for real."

"Trav, I can do it." She was all determination now. "You can count on me."

"That's what I needed to hear."

"Then, can we go in?"

"There's one more thing…"

"What?"

"It's important tomorrow night that you be on. You need to show them your most outgoing self. Sell your own personality." When she nodded up at him, he went on, "I did a lot of research on reality shows before I went into this. What I learned is that the show is a story, Bren. A story told in weekly episodes. And a good story is all about big personalities, characters you can't forget, over-the-top emotions. What I'm saying is, you can't be shy. It's better to embarrass yourself than to be all bottled up and boring. Are you hearing what I'm saying?"

"Yes, I am. And let me ask you something. When have you ever known me to be boring?"

Her various escapades over the years scrolled through his mind. At the age of nine, she'd gotten mad at her mom and run away. She got all the way to Portland, Oregon, before they caught up with her. At twelve, she'd coldcocked one of the Peabody boys when she caught him picking on a younger kid. Peabody hit the ground hard. It took thirty stitches to sew him back up. At sixteen, she'd rolled her pickup over a cliff because she never could resist a challenge and Leonie Parker had dared her to race up Falls Mountain. Only the good Lord knew how she'd survived that crash without major injury.

The more Travis thought of all the crazy things she'd done, the more certain he became that Brenna O'Reilly would have no problem selling herself to Giselle and the rest of them. "All right. I hear you."

"Good. 'Cause I'm a lot of things, Travis Dalton. But I am *never* shy or boring."

The next night, Real Deal Entertainment had assigned Gerry to drive the finalists to the Ace in the Hole.

All except for Travis. They let him make a quick trip to Kalispell in the afternoon and then, in the evening, he drove his F-150 out to the O'Reilly place to pick up his supposed fiancée.

Brenna's mom answered his knock. Travis had always liked Maureen O'Reilly. She loved her life on the family ranch, and her kitchen was the heart of her home. She'd always treated Travis with warmth and affection.

Tonight, however? Not so much. When he swept off his hat and gave her a big smile, she didn't smile back.

"Hello, Travis." Maureen pulled back the door and then hustled him into the living room, where she offered him a seat on the sofa. "Brenna will be right down."

"Great. Thanks."

She leaned toward him a little and asked in a low voice, "Travis, I need you to be honest with me. What's going on here?"

Before he left Brenna at the beauty shop yesterday, they'd agreed on how to handle things with her parents and his. Right now, Maureen needed to know that there was *something* going on between him and her middle daughter. The news of their engagement, however, would come a little bit later. "Brenna and I have a whole lot in common. She's agreed to come out to the audition at the Ace with me tonight."

"What does that mean, 'a whole lot in common'?"

"I care for her. I care for her deeply." It was surprisingly easy to say. Probably because it was true. He did care for Brenna. Always had. "She's one of a kind. There's no other girl like her."

Maureen scowled. She opened her mouth to speak again, but before she got a word out, her husband, Paddy, appeared in the archway that led to the kitchen.

"Travis. How you doin'?"

"Great, Paddy." He popped to his feet, and he and Paddy shook hands. "Real good to see you."

"Heard about you and that reality show."

"Final audition is tonight."

"Well, good luck to you, son."

Maureen started to speak again, but Brenna's arrival cut her off. "It's show business, Dad," she scolded with a playful smile. "In show business, you say 'break a leg.'"

Travis tried not to stare as she came down the stairs wearing dark-wash jeans that hugged her strong legs and a sleeveless lace-trimmed purple top that clung to every curve. Damn, she was fine. Purple suede dress boots and a rhinestone-studded cowboy hat completed the perfect picture she made.

Again, Travis reminded himself that she was spunky little Brenna O'Reilly and this so-called relationship they were going to have when they got on the show was just that—all show. Brenna didn't need to be messing with a troublesome cowboy like him.

And he knew very well that Maureen thought so, too.

Still, he could almost start having *real* ideas about Brenna and him and what they might get up to together pretending to be engaged during *The Great Roundup*.

Brenna kissed her mom on the cheek and then her dad, too. She handed Travis her rhinestone-trimmed jean jacket and he helped her into it.

They managed to get out the door and into the pickup without Maureen asking any more uncomfortable questions.

"It's time," she said in a low and angry tone as he turned off the dirt road from the ranch and onto the highway heading toward town. "Scratch that. It's *past* time I got my own place." Rentals in Rust Creek Falls were hard to come by. A lot of young women like Brenna lived with their parents until they got married or finally scraped together enough to buy something of their own. "Bee offered me her apartment over the beauty shop. She's been living in Kalispell, anyway, with her new guy. So when we win *The Great Roundup*, I'm moving. I love my mom, but she's driving me crazy."

"*When we win.* That's the spirit." As for Maureen, he played the diplomat. "Your mom's a wonderful woman."

Brenna shook her head and stared out the window. He almost asked her exactly what Maureen might have said to upset her—but then again, it was probably about him and he wasn't sure he wanted to know.

The rest of the ride passed in silence. Travis wanted to give Brenna a little more coaching on how to become a reality TV star, but the closer they got to town, the more withdrawn she seemed. He started to worry that something was really bothering her—something more than annoyance with her mom. And he had no idea what to say to ease whatever weighed on her mind.

The parking lot at the Ace was full. Music poured out of the ramshackle wooden building at the front of the lot. They were playing a fast one, something with a driving beat. Travis drove up and down the rows of parked vehicles, looking for a free space. Finally, in the last row at the very back of the lot, he found one.

He pulled in and turned off the engine. "You okay, Brenna?"

She aimed a blinding smile at him. "Great. Let's get going." Shoving open her door, she got out.

So he jumped out on his side and hustled around to her. He offered his hand. She gave him the strangest wild-eyed sort of look, but then she took it. Hers was ice-cold. He laced their fingers together and considered pulling her back, demanding to know if she was all right.

"Let's do this." She started walking, head high, that red hair shining down her back, rhinestones glittering on her hat, along the cuffs, hem and collar of her pretty denim jacket.

He fell in step with her, though he had a scary premonition they were headed straight for disaster. She seemed completely determined to go forward. He was afraid to slow her down, afraid that would finish her somehow, that calling a halt until she told him what was wrong would only make her turn and run. Their chance on *The Great Roundup* would be lost before they even got inside to try for it.

They went around to the front of the building and

up the wooden steps. A couple of cowboys came out and held the door for them. Both men looked at Brenna with interest, and Travis felt a buzz of irritation under his skin. He gave them each a warning glare. The men tipped their hats and kept on walking.

Inside, it was loud and wall-to-wall with partiers. Travis had never seen the Ace this packed. He spotted a couple of cameramen filming the crowd. Over by the bar, he caught sight of old Wally Wilson, a fellow finalist who'd grown up on the Oklahoma prairie and ridden the rodeos all over the West. Wally was talking the ear off one of the bartenders. And another finalist, that platinum blonde rodeo star, Summer Knight, was surrounded by cowboys. He knew it was her by the shine of her almost-white hair and that sexy laugh of hers.

"Come on." He pulled Brenna in closer so she could hear him. "We'll find the casting director, Giselle. I'll introduce you."

She blinked and stared at him through those now-enormous eyes. What was going on with her?

She looked terrified and he had no idea what to do about it.

Brenna *was* terrified.

She was totally freaking out. Brenna never freaked out.

And that freaked her out even more.

She'd been so sure she knew how to handle herself. She *did* know how to handle herself. She was bold. Fearless. Nothing scared her. Ever.

Except this, the Ace packed to bursting, the music so loud. All these people pressing in around her, a casting director waiting to meet her.

And Travis.

Travis, who was counting on her to win them both a spot on *The Great Roundup*.

Dear Lord, she didn't want to blow this. She would never forgive herself if she let Travis down.

"There's Giselle." Travis waved at a tall, model-skinny woman on the other side of the room. The woman lifted a hand and signaled them to join her. "This way." His fingers still laced with hers, he started working his way through the crowd, leading her toward the tall woman with cheekbones so sharp they threatened to poke right through her skin.

"Wait." Brenna dug in her boot heels.

He stopped and turned back to her, a worried frown between his eyebrows. "Bren?" He said her name softly, gently. He knew she was losing it. "What? Tell me."

She blasted a smile at him and forced a brittle laugh. "Can you just give me a minute?" She tipped her head toward the hallway that led to the ladies' room. "I'll be right back." She tugged free of his grip.

"Brenna—"

"I need to check my lip gloss."

"But —"

"Right back." She sent him a quick wave over her shoulder and made for the hallway, scattering *Excuse me*s as she went, weaving her way as fast as she could through the tight knots of people, ignoring anyone who spoke to her or glanced her way.

When she reached the hallway, she kept on going, her eyes on the glowing green exit sign down at the end. She got to the ladies' room and she didn't even slow down. She just kept right on walking down to the end of the hall.

And out the back door.

Chapter Three

The heavy door swung shut behind Brenna, and the racket from inside dimmed a little. She'd emerged into a loading area, with the packed dirt parking lot spread out beyond. Under the light of a few lamps on tall wooden poles, the rows of empty cars waited, not a soul in sight. Brenna shivered at the eeriness of it after the crush of people inside.

With no idea what to do next, she kept walking, her arms wrapped tightly around herself, her head tipped down, not knowing where she was going—until she ran right into someone coming the other way.

"Whoa, now…" said a raspy male voice.

She blinked and looked up—first at the dirty top half of a union suit. The shirt was frayed around the wattled neck of an old man with bristly gray whiskers and thinning, scraggly white hair. "Homer," she said in a dazed whisper. "Homer Gilmore."

The old man smiled, showing crooked, yellowed teeth. "If it isn't Brenna O'Reilly. Where you headin' in such an all-fired hurry?"

"I was just…"

"Runnin' away?" he finished for her.

Homer was famous in Rust Creek Falls for a number of reasons. He made moonshine that made people throw off their inhibitions. He tended to show up when you least expected him. And he *knew* things. Travis might scoff at her for saying it, but that didn't make it any less true. Homer really could read things about people. He always seemed to know intuitively what folks were going through.

She started to deny that she was running anywhere. "I was just—"

"Scared, is what you were. And that is not like you."

"I got—"

"Stage fright. I know. Sometimes it happens."

"Homer, how do you—"

"Know things?" He only laughed, a sound every bit as ragged and rusty as the rest of him. And then he lowered his head. Brenna followed his gaze to his gnarled right hand, in which he held a jar of clear liquid.

"Homer, is that—"

"Just what you need about now? Yeah, Brenna. It is."

She looked up into his watery eyes again. "But I don't want to get—"

"Drunk? Uh-uh. You won't be. This is just a little magic for you, that's all. A little nudge in the right direction for this one time. Look at me, Brenna." His voice was softer now. She could just wrap it around her, it sounded so soothing and good. She looked right into his eyes.

"Say what you're thinking," he instructed.

And she did. "I'm still afraid, but it's okay. I'm bigger than my fear."

"That's right. That's the spirit." He held out the jar. "Take one long drink, Brenna O'Reilly. And then get back in there and show them what you're made of."

She took the jar and unscrewed the lid.

Travis was getting really worried.

And not only about the fact that Giselle kept shooting him dirty looks and mouthing, "Where *is* she?" across the crowded dance floor at him.

He was worried about Brenna. She'd looked so upset when she took off for the restroom. He shouldn't have let her go like that. He should have gone with her, made sure she got there safe, made sure she was okay.

She'd seemed so cocky and confident yesterday, so completely *Brenna*, out there behind the beauty shop. He'd really believed she could handle anything *The Great Roundup* could throw at her. So he'd gotten her into this.

Travis had pulled some crazy stunts in his life, but one thing he'd always done right was to look out for Brenna O'Reilly. He'd protected her from more than one potential disaster.

Not tonight, though. Something was really bothering her, and he knew it. And still, he'd let her leave his side.

It was an error in judgment on his part, and he needed to rectify that. He needed to stop standing here like a damn fool and go after her.

He started for the hallway that led to the restrooms. People pushed in around him, and he just pushed back. Nodding, forcing a smile when anyone spoke to him, he kept going until he reached the hallway, where a line of women waited to get into the restroom. Brenna was not among them.

He was just trying to decide whether or not to barge into the ladies' room shouting her name when the door all the way down at the end of the hallway opened— and there she was.

"Brenna!"

She tipped her chin high so he could see her face clearly under the brim of her hat. She spotted him— and she smiled, a bright, glowing smile. Hot damn, she was gorgeous.

And apparently, she'd gotten over whatever had been bothering her.

"Travis!" She gave him a jaunty wave and started toward him.

"'Scuse me, ladies." He eased his way between two women at the front of the restroom line and went for her, not stopping till he stood in front of her a few feet from the door. "Brenna, are you okay?"

She grinned up at him. "Never better." She really did seem fine now, brimming with her usual bright confidence.

But he had to be sure. He leaned close and said for her ears alone, "We don't have to do this. I can take you home."

She reached up and got a handful of the front of his shirt. "We're not giving up now. Don't even think it."

"But are you —"

She cut him off by jerking him down to her and lifting her mouth to within an inch from his. "We are doing this." Her eyes had stars in them. "And we are taking home the prize."

"Brenna…" She smelled of flowers and fresh-cut grass. He really wanted to kiss her.

"Do it," she whispered, clearly reading his mind. "We need to do it. How can we pretend that we're headed for forever when you've never even put your lips on mine?"

Was she right? Did he really *need* to kiss her to make their fake relationship seem real for Giselle and the others? Hell if he knew. All he could think was that he'd never kissed her—and he *had* to kiss her.

Finally. At last.

He lowered his head a fraction closer, and she surged up.

His mouth touched hers.

With a sigh, she let go of his shirtfront and her hands slid up to clasp the back of his neck. "Travis…" She stroked his nape with her soft fingers as she whispered his name, kissing it onto his lips.

So good. So right. She tasted of honey, of ripe summer fruit—peaches and blackberries, watermelon. Cherries. She tasted of promises, sweet hopes and big dreams. She tasted of home.

Someone up the hall a ways let out a whoop, while someone else yelled, "Kiss her, cowboy!"

Neither Travis nor Brenna paid their hecklers any mind. The brims of their hats collided as they deepened the kiss. His fell and then hers, but neither of them cared.

That kiss went on forever.

And still, it was too short.

She ended it, finally, by dropping back down to her heels again. Dazed, reluctant to lose the hot spell of her kiss, he opened his eyes to find her staring up at him, her mouth as plump and red as the cherries she tasted like.

"Brenna…" he whispered like some kind of long-gone fool. At that moment, her name was the only word he knew.

She gave a low laugh and dipped to the floor, grabbing both their hats and passing him his. He slid it on his head as she held out her hand. "Come on, cowboy. Let's go have ourselves some fun."

How did she do it?

Travis had no idea.

But that night, Brenna was a natural, a reality TV show dream come true.

He took her to Giselle first. She shook Giselle's hand, leaned in close and whispered something.

Giselle laughed out loud. In the weeks he'd been dealing with her, Travis had never seen Giselle laugh.

It went on like that all night. Brenna was sexy and funny and so good at pretending to be in love with him, he almost believed it himself. She rubbed up against him and pulled him down to whisper naughty things in his ear. And the way she smiled at him? You'd have thought he was the only guy in the place.

All the other guys wanted to dance with her, but Travis kept her close. After the way he'd lost her there at first, he wasn't letting her out of his sight again tonight.

She was so relaxed and easy, mugging for the cameras, but not too much. Just enough to be charming and playful and fun. She was drinking Coca-Cola, hadn't had a single beer. Still, he couldn't help wondering if she'd knocked back a little liquid courage when he wasn't looking.

Once he even whispered, "Are you drunk?"

She laughed that magical, joyful laugh of hers. And then she kissed him—a deep, wet, amazing kiss that made him acutely aware of exactly how long it had been since he'd had sex with a woman.

And the way she felt in his arms when they danced?

So good. Just right. He could almost start wishing the night would never end.

At a little past midnight, with the band on a break, Giselle signaled them over again. She had two of the cameramen with her that time.

Travis knew what the casting director was up to. They were getting interviewed, an on-the-fly interview to test them both, to see if they had chemistry up close and personal, and to find out if Brenna could really shine with the camera focused right on her.

Giselle asked, "Brenna, how long have you two been together?"

Travis wanted to grab her and whisper that no matter what, she was amazing. If they made it or not, he'd owe her forever for this fine night at the Ace.

But then Brenna laughed. And he knew that she had them. "How long have Travis and I been together? Not nearly long enough, if you ask me." She grabbed his arm and snuggled up close. "I have loved Travis Dalton since I was six years old," she said dreamily. "That was the day that my mom let me ride my new bike on the Cedar Street sidewalk while she was shopping at Crawford's General Store. It was the day that Angus McCauley pushed me off my bike and then rode away on it. I called Angus some bad names, but he didn't come back. So I sat down on the sidewalk and burst into tears…"

It seemed to Travis at that moment that the whole

place had gone quiet. People pressed close, but only so they could hear better as Brenna told them how Travis had appeared out of nowhere that day.

"He came like a knight in shining armor—except, you know, in dusty boots, jeans and a snap-front shirt." She looked up at him with a glowing smile.

He brushed her lips with his, the light kiss so easy and natural, exactly right. He looked at the nearest camera. "I hate to see a little girl cry."

Brenna went on with her story. "He picked me up and asked me if I was hurt. I showed him the scrape on my elbow where I'd hit the sidewalk when Angus pushed me down. Travis looked at it, all serious and frowning. He said, 'You are a very brave little girl. Stay right here. I'll get your bike.' And he did just that. Not five minutes later, he came back around the corner of Cedar and North Buckskin Road, walking my bike. I ran to meet him, and that was when I told him I loved him and would marry him someday."

"What did he say to that?" Giselle asked downright breathlessly.

Brenna let out a put-upon sigh. "He acted like I hadn't said it. He did that a lot for the next twenty years or so."

"She was too young for me," Travis insisted, as he'd done more than once during the twenty years in question.

Brenna made a face at him. "The second time I said I loved him, I was eight and he was sixteen. That time, as it so happened, he'd just saved me from drowning in Rust Creek. I said, 'Oh, Travis. I love you and I can't wait to marry you!' He just wrapped me in a blanket and drove me home. And then, when I was ten…"

He knew what was coming and couldn't hold back a groan.

She nudged him with her shoulder. "Aurelia won't mind. Remember, she got married and moved to Sioux Falls?"

Giselle, looking more eager than Travis had ever seen her, prompted, "So tell us what happened."

"I caught them kissing, Travis and Aurelia."

"Oh, no!" Gerry, the production assistant who stood at Giselle's elbow, gave Travis a dirty look.

"Oh, yes," said Brenna. "And okay, I was only ten, but still it destroyed me. It was in the summer, out at the county rodeo. Aurelia and Travis were both eighteen. Aurelia was so annoying. She had breasts and everything. I took one look at the two of them squishing their mouths together and felt my poor heart break clean in two."

"Heartbreak?" Travis teased her. "Come on, admit it, Brenna. You were mad, not heartbroken."

She gave a sniff, her cute nose in the air. "That was not anger, that was pure heartbreak, just like I said. Heartbreak that caused me to pick up a rock and throw it at Aurelia. I hit her in the shoulder."

Travis elaborated, "Aurelia let out a yelp you could hear all the way to Kalispell." He scolded Brenna gently, "You hit her pretty hard."

"Well, I was upset and it seemed to me at the time that she deserved it."

He shook his head. "You always did have a good arm on you, even when you were ten."

"I remember she called me an evil little brat. And I turned to you and said, 'Travis Dalton, what is the matter with you? You're supposed to be waiting for *me*.' I reminded you that I was already ten and it wouldn't be long now—or it wouldn't *have* been."

"Except that you were so mad—"

"Correction. Brokenhearted. I was so *brokenhearted*, I ended it between us."

"Bren. Come on. You were *ten*. I was eighteen. There was nothing to end."

She put her finger to his lips. "Shh. *I'm* tellin' this story." And then she spoke to the camera again. "I said that on second thought, I hated him and I wasn't going to marry him, after all, no matter if he crawled on his knees to me through razor blades and broken glass."

He leaned in and told the camera confidentially, "She was always a bloodthirsty little thing."

"Maybe. Now and then." Brenna let out a rueful sigh. "Especially when the guy I love goes and breaks my heart." Slowly, she grinned. "But then, look at us now." She grabbed Travis closer. He went willingly. "Travis Dalton, I forgive you."

"For...?"

"Not taking me seriously when I was six and breaking my poor heart when I was ten."

He would have delivered a clever comeback for that one, but she went and offered up her sweet mouth. Comebacks could wait. He claimed her lips in another long, bone-melting kiss that brought a volley of applause and appreciative laughter from the circle of contestants and locals surrounding them.

When he lifted his head, she said, "Finally together, forever and over."

It was the perfect moment, the one Travis had been waiting for.

He dropped to his knees, reached in his pocket and

took out the ring he'd slipped in there before driving out to the O'Reilly place to pick her up that night. That ring, bought in Kalispell that afternoon, had cost him more than half of his hard-earned savings. But he'd spent that money anyway, because the ring was as beautiful as she was and because it was important that they come across as the real thing.

"Travis!" Brenna stared down at him through shining ocean-blue eyes. "Oh, Travis..." Those fine eyes shone even brighter with her tears. Damn, she was amazing. "That is the most beautiful ring I have ever seen."

"I was hoping you might think so." And he really was getting into this, maybe more than he should. "Brenna O'Reilly," he said with feeling, "I love you and you are the only woman in the world for me."

"Oh, Trav. I love you, too."

God. The way she looked at him. He didn't care if it was all an act. Nothing lit him up like the glory of her smile. "Marry me, Brenna."

"Yes, Travis. Yes!"

"Hot damn!" He slipped the ring on her finger, jumped to his feet and threw his hat in the air. Everyone with a hat followed suit. Hats went flying everywhere. To a thundering rumble of excited applause and a torrent of catcalls and triumphant shouts, Travis grabbed Brenna close in his arms and kissed her again for all he was worth.

"Brenna," Giselle said as soon as Travis and Brenna had been congratulated by half the partiers in the place, "you think you could give us a few minutes alone?"

Brenna looked a little stunned. She turned to Travis. "Trav?"

He slid his hand down and clasped hers. "I'll go with you."

Giselle gave a shrug. "Suit yourselves." She pointed her index finger at the ceiling. "One moment." The finger dipped down. "Do not move from this spot." She turned and consulted with two of the cameramen, putting her eye to one viewfinder and then the other, evidently checking out footage that had already been shot. Then she gestured at various contestants around the Ace. The cameramen moved off, seeking their assigned targets. "All right then," said Giselle. "This way, you two."

The band started up again as Travis and Brenna followed the casting director and her assistant to the long hall that led to the back door. Giselle took them past the restrooms, finally opening the last door before the one that led out. "Here we go." She ushered them into a small space with a desk, a battered couch and two chairs. Apparently, she'd made arrangements to have the room available.

The pounding beat of the music receded to a dull roar as Giselle shut the door. She gestured for Travis and Brenna to take the two guest chairs while she claimed the big chair behind the desk. Roxanne, with one of those tablet phones, took the minion position at Giselle's shoulder, stylus at the ready.

"I'll get right to the point." Giselle rocked back in the chair. "Brenna, the camera loves you. And we like you. We like you a lot." She held up her thumb and index finger with a half inch of space between them. "You're this far from being on *The Great Roundup*—both you and your handsome fiancé here."

Bren felt for his hand again. He grabbed hers and held on tight.

Giselle asked wryly, "So, am I safe in assuming that you *are* interested in being on the show?"

Brenna's head bobbed up and down. "I am interested. Definitely."

"We'll have to arrange for some other test footage— what we would have wanted to see in your package. Can you ride a horse?"

"Oh, yes, I can."

"How about roping?"

"I was raised on a ranch. I'm not a champion roper, but I have the basics down."

"Well, all right then, it can all be arranged. We're going to put you up at Maverick Manor with Travis and the rest of the finalists. There will be contracts to sign, more interviews and a series of tests and a background check."

"Yes. I'm ready."

"You're saying you're in?"

"Yes, I am." Bren straightened her shoulders. "I want to do this."

"All right, then." Giselle gave a slow nod. "You're ours. You would potentially be here in Rust Creek Falls at Maverick Manor for a couple of weeks. And then, if you're chosen for the final cast, you'll go on location until filming is complete."

Brenna squeezed Travis's hand. "I want to do it."

"Wonderful." Giselle doled out one of those almost smiles of hers.

Brenna raised her free hand—like a kid in class getting permission to speak. "But…"

"Go on."

"Well, I need to go home tonight. I could be at the Manor by noon tomorrow, if that's all right. But first I need a little time with my family. I need to catch them up on all that's, um, going on."

Giselle sat back in her chair and rocked a moment. "All right. Go home, talk to the family and pack your bags. We'll expect you at Maverick Manor at twelve noon tomorrow, to stay."

"I'll be back tomorrow, early, to talk to your folks and then to drive you to the Manor," Travis said.

Brenna sat with him in his pickup in front of the ranch house. All the windows were dark. Her mom had left the porch light on, though. It cast a golden pool of light that reached to the bottom of the front steps. Beyond that, the night took over.

Brenna touched the stone of her gorgeous engagement ring. Even in the dark, it glittered. They weren't really engaged, but still, the ring already seemed to her like a good-luck charm. The feel of it on her finger soothed her somehow. "I can tell them about the engagement on my own. You don't need to be here for that."

"Are you kidding? Your dad and brothers would come looking for me with blood in their eyes if I wasn't there with you to share the big news."

"Oh, come on. They would not."

"I should be there. I *will* be there."

"Travis, stop. It's not even real."

"But they have to *believe* it's real. You know that."

Her throat felt tight. She coughed into her hand to clear it. "Okay. I know you're right. But are you sure you can leave the Manor again? Don't they *own* you, like Giselle said?"

"Bren…" He reached out as though he would touch her, caress her—but then he caught himself and dropped his hand. She couldn't help wishing he'd carried through. This pretending to be engaged to him was pretty confusing. Already, she found it too easy to forget that it wasn't real. "They're giving me a little leeway," he explained. "Because they want both of us and I'm helping them to get you on the show." He took her hand and cradled it between his two big rough ones. "Are you having second thoughts?"

She whipped her hand free and bopped him lightly on his rock-hard chest. "No, I am not. No way. I *want* this job, and I aim to get it."

He gave her his sexiest grin. "That's what I needed to hear. Come on, I'll walk you in."

"It's not necess—"

"Shh. Don't say that. Of course it's necessary. You're my bride-to-be, and I am the luckiest man on the planet. A lucky man like me is honored to walk his girl to her front door."

That did make her chuckle. "I think you could charm the habit off a nun."

"Brenna, you know I would never do such a thing— because that would be disrespectful to a woman of God. And because I am already spoken for."

"Oh, Travis. You've got one silver tongue on you."

"Stay right there."

"Why?"

"I'll come around and open your door."

She laughed again and shook her head at him. But she waited, let him walk around the front of his crew cab, pull her door wide and offer his hand. She took it and felt like a queen as he helped her down.

They went up the front steps and stood under the porch light.

He leaned close, bringing his manly scent of soap and leather and a hint of pine. "I think I should kiss you. And I think you should let me."

"And why is that?" she whispered back.

"We're engaged, remember? An engaged man will always kiss his sweetheart good-night." He'd left his hat in the pickup, and the porch light cast his eyes into darkness, gave a bronze sheen to his almost-black hair.

"But, Travis, we're only engaged when someone is looking."

He tipped up her chin. "And you never know, someone could be watching us right now. We can't be too careful." His lips brushed hers, so lightly, back and forth. His beard, which he kept trimmed short enough that it bordered on scruff, scratched a little in the sexiest sort of way.

Too soon, he lifted his head.

She longed to grab him, pull him in closer, demand a *real* kiss good-night.

But she didn't. It *wasn't* real, and she had to remember that.

She heard whining on the other side of the door. Her mom's dog, Duchess. She needed to go in before the dog started barking. "See you tomorrow."

"I'll be here at eight." Everyone would be up long before that. On a working ranch, a lot got done before breakfast. "Don't say a word until I get here."

"Oh, please. It's Rust Creek Falls. Remember, you live here? Everyone is bound to be talking about what happened at the Ace tonight. You took a knee and I took your beautiful ring. That's huge news. Somebody's probably already called my mom."

"In the middle of the night?"

"As if the gossip grapevine keeps regular hours. Besides, she has a cell phone. Someone could have texted her. She gets up at five. One look at her phone and she'll be pounding on my bedroom door."

"Don't be so negative. It's all going to be fine."

"Oh, Travis. I really hope you're right."

"How about this? I'll be out here in my truck at 5:00 a.m., ready whenever you need me."

Now she wanted to grab him and kiss him again for being willing to do that—but no. It wouldn't be right to ask that of him. "Are you crazy? It's already after two."

"Good point. So I might as well just stay. I'll be right over there." He pointed at his waiting pickup. "It won't be the first time I slept in my truck. Then I can run in and rescue you when your mom starts yelling."

"You act like it's a joke, but you know my mother. She's got the biggest heart in the county, but she likes things slow and steady. You and me and what we are up to? About as far from slow and steady as anyone can get."

"I'll be here. Don't worry."

"No. That's not right. I shouldn't have said anything. Eight o'clock is fine. Now go on." She put on a smile and made shooing motions with her hands. "Go back to the Manor and get some sleep."

Just to make sure he didn't stay anyway, she waited to go in until she'd watched him drive off.

A volley of sharp taps jarred Brenna awake.

And then her mom's voice demanded, "Brenna O'Reilly, open this door."

Brenna groaned and put her pillow over her head. "Go away, Mom."

"Open. Now. I mean it!"

Brenna peeked out from under her pillow at the bedside clock—4:55 a.m.

Her mother knocked again. Loudly. "I need to talk to you. Open this door now!"

No doubt about it. Her mother had heard the big news.

Chapter Four

"Brenna!"

"Ugh. Fine." Brenna threw back the covers, stalked to the door and yanked it wide. "What?"

"I just got a call from Mary Dalton. She wanted to know if I knew that you and Travis got engaged last night."

Brenna raked her tangled hair off her forehead and leaned on the door frame. "Mom. Can you just calm down a little, please?"

"I'm perfectly calm!"

"You don't seem very—"

"Oh, Brenna," her mother cried and grabbed the hand Brenna had just used to push her hair back. Maureen made a strangled sound as she gaped at the ring Travis had slipped on her finger last night. "It's…beautiful." Maureen's voice trembled, threatening tears.

Brenna gently pulled her hand free. "Mom," she said softly. She started to reach for a hug.

But Maureen nipped that impulse in the bud. "Travis?" she demanded. "Honestly? I mean, I know he's handsome and charming and all the girls love him. I know you've had a crush on him since you were practically in diapers, but...*Travis*?"

Brenna felt annoyance rise again. She straightened and folded her arms across the extra large Bushwacker T-shirt she wore for a nightgown. "You don't have to say his name like that. It's just rude."

"Rude? You're engaged to Travis Dalton out of the blue and *I'm* being rude? This is so..." Maureen ran out of words, but then quickly regrouped. "This is everything you've been saying you weren't going to do anymore. It's impulsive and crazy and— Oh, Brenna. You promised. After Juárez, you said you'd learned your lesson at last."

Juárez. Brenna felt a stab of shame, though what had happened there wasn't really her fault. Still, Juárez had been awful, and her dad had had to come and bail her out of jail. After Juárez, she really had been trying to keep a lid on her natural propensity to end up in situations that some might call risky.

But this wasn't risky. This was actually about settling down, about owning her own business and getting her own place. And no way was she letting it slip through her fingers.

Her mother wasn't finished. "What about working hard and keeping both feet on the ground? What about learning to look before you leap? Travis Dalton is a great guy and I'm very fond of him, you know that.

Who wouldn't be? But we both know he's not a settling-down kind of man."

"Mom. I love you," she said through clenched teeth. "I've made some mistakes and I admit that I have. But I'm also twenty-six years old and perfectly capable of making my own decisions about how to run my life."

Her mother opened her mouth to argue some more—but then her dad called up the stairs, "Maureen, Brenna! Travis is here."

Brenna stiffened. How much had the men heard—and had poor Trav slept outside in his truck, after all?

Maureen shut her mouth over whatever she had been going to say. And then she called down, "We're coming!"

Brenna yanked on a pair of jeans and followed her mother down to the front hall.

Her dad must have come in from doing his morning chores. In stocking feet, he stood by the door with Travis, who wore the same clothes he'd had on last night. Both men looked really uncomfortable. Yep. No doubt about it. They'd heard what had been said upstairs.

Brenna went right to Travis. Why shouldn't she? They were supposed to be engaged, after all. He put his arm around her. She leaned into his warmth and strength and liked being there probably more than she should have. "You didn't go back to the Manor, did you?" she chided.

He kissed the end of her nose. She loved that—even if the gesture did cause her mother to suck in a sharp breath. "I drove around the first bend in the driveway and waited for you to go in," he confessed.

"You shouldn't have."

"I wanted to be here. And I think it's a good thing

I stayed." He squeezed her shoulder, pulling her even tighter into the circle of his arm. And then he faced her parents. "Maureen, Paddy, I guess you've already figured out that Brenna has made me the happiest man alive and agreed to be my wife. I realize this might seem a little sudden, but—"

"A *little* sudden?" Maureen sniffed.

Travis didn't miss a beat. "I love your daughter and I hope you will see it in your hearts to wish us well." Dear Lord, the man was *good*. He should have been an actor, no doubt about it.

Her dad, always an easier sell than her mother, gave a slow nod. "Well, now." He hooked his arm around her mom. "It's never too early in the morning for good news, right, darlin'?"

"Oh, Paddy." Her mother elbowed him gently in the side. She let out a tired-sounding sigh. "Let's all go on in the kitchen. I'll make some coffee and we can talk."

"Good idea," said her dad. With a hard huff of a sigh, her mom left them. That was when Paddy took a step forward and offered Travis his hand. They shook. "You be good to my girl, now."

"I will, sir. You have my word on it."

Her dad held out his arms. Brenna went into them, feeling dewy eyed and grateful to both of her parents. Her mom could drive her crazy, but there'd never been any shortage of love in the O'Reilly house. "You be happy," Paddy whispered in her ear. "You hear me?"

"I love you, Dad. So much." She hugged him back, good and tight.

Ten minutes later the four of them sat around the old kitchen table, each with a comforting mug of morning coffee to sip. Too soon, her older sister, Fiona, would be coming downstairs and her brothers, Ronan and Keegan, would appear from the barn, ready for breakfast.

Brenna wanted to tell her parents her other news before her siblings joined them. Travis must have been thinking the same thing, because when she glanced his way, he threw her an opening.

"I suppose you've both heard that I've made the finals in the national auditions for *The Great Roundup...*"

Brenna's mom looked a little pinched around the mouth. "Lately it seems like that show is all anybody in town ever talks about."

"Everyone's excited about it," said her dad.

If only Fallon were there. Brenna missed her younger sister desperately right then. Fallon had always understood her, was always on her side. But just a week before, Fallon had married the love of her life, Jamie Stockton. Fallon, Jamie and his adorable triplet toddlers were all off in Florida on a Disney World honeymoon.

Travis kept sending her questioning looks, waiting for her to either share her news or signal that she wanted him to do it. He was being much too wonderful, but she needed to step up and deal.

She drew a deep breath. "Mom. Dad. We have something else we, um, can't wait to tell you." She tried to inject excitement into her voice, but somehow it came out sounding squeaky and scared.

And why shouldn't she be scared? Running off for weeks to do *The Great Roundup* was every bit as wild and outrageous a plan as suddenly getting engaged to Travis. It fell squarely into the Brenna Does More Crazy Things category.

Her mother would not be thrilled.

A frown creased Maureen's brow. "What now?"

Brenna made herself say it. "It just so happens I'm a finalist to be on *The Great Roundup*, too."

Her mother sat very still. She did not say a word. Her dad knocked back a big gulp of coffee.

Swiftly, eager to get it over with now, Brenna told them what had happened at the Ace in the Hole the night before—that not only had Travis proposed, the casting director had said Brenna would be perfect for the show. "And so I'm moving to Maverick Manor for the next week or two. There will be more interviews before I find out for certain if I've made the final cast list."

"B-but what about your *job*?" her mom sputtered.

"Bee says she'll hold my booth for me."

"But this is just crazy." Maureen had more questions. A thousand of them.

Brenna answered them patiently.

Until her mom finally just gave up. "You'll do what you want to do. You always have." Wearily, as though she bore the weight of the world on her shoulders, Maureen pushed herself to her feet. "Let's get the breakfast started. You'll at least have a last home-cooked meal before you run off with Travis to be on TV."

At a little after eight, way ahead of schedule, Brenna's suitcases were packed and stowed in Travis's truck. Her older sister and brothers had all wished her well and she and Travis were on the road, headed for a stop at the Dalton Ranch before surrendering to the watchful custody of Giselle and crew.

"You're way too quiet." Travis glanced over at her.

She put on a wobbly smile for him. "It's my mother.

I love her so much, but there's just not enough room in that house for the both of us. I need my own place."

"And you'll get it when we win *The Great Roundup*." He took her hand, tugged it across the console and pressed his lips to the back of it. She didn't pull away. So what if no one was watching? His lips were so warm and his short beard felt silky, but a little scratchy, too. He made everything better, always had. He said, "All things considered, I thought it went well."

Shaking her head, she took her hand back. "You always did look on the bright side."

"That's me. Chock-full of happy thoughts."

She admired the ring he'd given her. How could she help it? "I know you spent way too much on this ring."

"You're worth it."

"I give up." She let her head fall against the seat back. "There's just no wrecking your positive attitude."

He laughed, a deep, manly sound that sent a sweet little shiver dancing all through her. "Come on. Your eyes are sparkling as bright as that ring you're wearing. You know as well I do that what we're doing…well, it's who we are. We're the ones who take the dares, the ones who go for the gold ring against all the odds. This is what we were born to do. And your mom? No matter how much she begs you to be someone you're not, she loves you for your guts and your gumption. Don't you doubt for a minute that she loves how you shine."

Brenna's throat clutched at his words. "Trav. That was beautiful."

"It's only the truth." He turned the truck into the long driveway that led to his parents' house. "Now brace yourself. We'll deal with my family and then we'll head for Maverick Manor, where the room service is 24/7 and all the mattresses have pillow tops. If you're lucky, you'll get to sneak in a nap before Giselle comes knocking, ready to make you a star."

The visit with Ben and Mary Dalton went pretty well. If Travis's parents had their doubts about this engagement, they also had the grace to keep it to themselves. There were hugs and well-wishing all around.

Ben said, "Proud of you, son."

Mary warned, "You'd better treat this sweet girl right."

Travis wrapped his arm around Brenna, pressed a kiss to her temple and promised that he would.

At Maverick Manor, Gerry had already arranged for Brenna's room —next to Travis's, with an adjoining door between. "Because we know you two will want to be close." Gerry mimed a racing heartbeat with a hand against his chest—and then burst into "People Will Say We're in Love" from *Oklahoma.*

He belted out two verses, standing right there in the hallway. And then he blushed. "Musical theater. Always my first love. I played Curly at Kansas City Rep back before I decided to move to LA." He drew his shoulders back. "I may not be tall, but I have a tall presence. I mean, Tom Cruise is only five-seven, right?"

"Right." Brenna gave him a big smile. "And your voice is amazing."

"Thank you." Gerry granted her a regal nod. Then he stuck the key card in the reader and swung the door wide. "Milady. Your chamber awaits."

Brenna put her stuff in the drawers and then fell across the wide bed. It was a pillow top, just as Travis had promised. She kicked off her boots, closed her eyes and slept for five full hours—until Travis tapped on the door between their rooms.

She let him in and they ordered room service. As they ate, he gave her more tips on how to handle Giselle, what kind of footage they were going to want on her and what to say at her psych evaluation.

The next days were busy ones. Brenna rode a horse and roped a calf for the cameras. She gave more interviews and Skyped with network executives. She met the other finalists and liked most of them, especially Roberta Hinckes, who was in her midforties and coming off a bad divorce from some corporate bigwig who'd dumped her for his executive assistant. Tall and slim with thick brown hair, Roberta was not only levelheaded and smart, she was gorgeous. The guy who'd traded her in for a younger model had to be a complete fool.

Travis, meanwhile, made friends with Steve Simons, who had lost a leg from the knee down in Iraq. The former soldier was black and heartthrob handsome. He'd just turned thirty. The four of them—Travis and Brenna, Roberta and Steve—hung out every chance they got.

On Friday, six days after Brenna first checked in at the Manor, all forty-six finalists were ordered down to the conference room. Twenty were sent packing.

Travis, Brenna, Steve and Roberta, along with Wally Wilson and Summer Knight, the rodeo star, were among the twenty-six finalists still in the running.

Travis touched the back of Brenna's hand. She laced her fingers with his and held on tight. They were so close now. Only four more finalists would be eliminated. Brenna just knew that she and Trav would both make the cut. She felt it in her bones.

"I won't congratulate any of you yet," said the field producer, Roger DelRay, who would be going with the final cast when they left for location to begin filming. "We'll be meeting with a few of you privately to discuss certain necessary contract clauses before the final four cuts can be made."

Brenna leaned close to Travis. "'Necessary contract clauses'? What does that even mean?"

"Got me."

When Roger dismissed them, Giselle's assistant grabbed Brenna's arm as she and Travis were following the others out of the conference room. "This way, you two," Roxanne said. "We have a few things we need to go over with you."

Brenna kept hold of Travis's hand as Roxanne led them into a smaller meeting room. Giselle, Roger DelRay and another producer were there, along with a tall, intense-looking bearded guy Brenna hadn't met before. There were blue file folders waiting on the table in front of two of the chairs.

"Welcome, you two," said Roger. "We would like you to meet Anthony Locke. He'll be directing *The Great Roundup*."

Anthony Locke shook their hands. "Let's have a seat, shall we?"

Giselle led them to the chairs in front of the blue folders.

"Travis, Brenna," said Locke, "we're all beyond sold. You each have the skill sets to excel in the challenges that will face you in the show—which means you each have a good chance to stay in the game once filming is under way. The camera loves both of you, and your chemistry together is off the charts. We want you both."

We're in! Brenna groped for Travis's hand again. As his strong fingers closed around hers, she somehow managed to suppress a gleeful shout of triumph.

"So let's get right down to business here," said Roger. "Your contracts are in front of you. Most of what you'll find there isn't going to surprise you. Travis, you've already signed your confidentiality agreement. Brenna, we'll need one from you, and it's in the folder before you."

Travis had already explained to her that all the contestants had to agree to total confidentiality concerning the show until after the last episode aired at the end of the year. That meant that even when filming ended and they all went home, they still wouldn't be able to tell anyone what had happened during shooting. No one could know who won, who lost, who came close—not until the series played out on national TV.

"I understand about the confidentiality clause," said Brenna.

"Excellent," said Roger. "And I'm sure you're both wondering why we've called you in together."

Travis made a low sound in the affirmative. Brenna nodded.

Roger smiled indulgently. "The truth is, you two have an extra clause in your contract that none of the other contestants will have to sign. It's on page twelve. We'll need you to take the agreement to your rooms with you and read it over carefully. You would both have to sign the clause, so talk it over with each other. Should either of you be eliminated early, the clause will most likely not be activated." Roger gave a smug little snort. "Because, frankly, if you're eliminated early, who's gonna care? Thus you'll note that the clause is activated at the sole discretion of Real Deal Entertainment. Meaning we decide to activate. Or not."

Brenna wasn't getting it. She sent Travis a sideways glance. He looked as confused as she felt.

Roger kept talking. "On a brighter note, if you both last on the show, if you both keep coming out ahead in the challenges, if we feel, as filming continues, that America will end up falling as hard for you young love-birds as we at Real Deal have, then we're throwing you a wedding." He beamed at them proudly.

Brenna almost choked. "Urgh," she squeaked. "Did you just say...a wedding?"

"Yes, you heard me right, Brenna. If all goes as we hope it will, you and Travis will be married on camera at the end of the show."

Chapter Five

Married?

They would have to get married on the show?

A numbness stole through Brenna.

No. She couldn't do it.

It was one thing to pretend they were engaged. An engagement, after all, could be broken by a simple and private decision, just between two people. With an engagement, all you had to say was that it didn't work out.

But marriage? A real, legal marriage, before God and a national audience? To break a marriage, you had to do a lot more than just decide to call it off. They would have to divorce each other. Or at least get an annulment.

Yeah, okay, she'd made a few questionable choices in her life, but she'd always been absolutely certain that when she got married, it would be forever. She might be the wild child of her family, but she still shared a bedrock foundation of O'Reilly family values.

A temporary marriage was simply a bridge too far.

Her stomach felt hollowed out, and her brain refused to function. She tried to pull her hand free of Travis's hold.

He didn't let go. He said to Roger and the others, "We would need to talk to our lawyer first."

Our lawyer? What lawyer? Brenna didn't have a lawyer. Or did he mean his dad, Ben, who ran a law office in town?

Bad idea. Ben, like the rest of Trav's family and hers, thought that she and Travis were *really* engaged. It wasn't right to put their secret on poor Ben. She sent Travis a frantic look. He gazed back at her steadily. Cool as they came

Brenna got the message. If she was going to freak out, she should do it in private. First rule of reality TV. save the drama for the cameras and never let the suits see you sweat.

Was that two rules?

Whatevs.

And okay. Maybe not Ben, but seeing a lawyer for this problem wasn't a bad idea. Some of the other finalists were pros at the reality show game. They had agents and lawyers advising them on their every move. Well, she and Travis had a right to a little legal advice, too— like how bad would it be to sign the marriage clause and then not follow through if it came to that?

She sucked in a slow breath and put on her game face. "Yes." She backed Travis up. "Our lawyer would have to advise us on something like this."

Roger nodded. "That's wise. Call in your attorney. We'll need your decision by tomorrow at noon."

They took their blue folders and went straight upstairs from the meeting. Brenna wanted to break something. She wanted to throw back her head and let out a scream.

Travis followed her into her room. The second the door clicked shut, she whirled on him. "We can't get married, and no way are we calling your dad about this."

"Bren," he said, using a soft, coaxing tone suitable for soothing riled horses. "Slow down. First things first."

She eyed him sideways, ready to bolt. "What things?"

He tipped his head at the small table by the window. "We sit down, we read what it says on page twelve and then we discuss."

She glared. "Discuss? There's nothing to discuss. We're not getting fake married, because you *can't* get fake married. If we get married on *The Great Roundup*, it will be for real and then we'll end up having to get a divorce. Trav, I don't want to be someone who's gotten divorced. Especially not when I haven't even *really* been married."

Instead of answering her, he turned and walked away.

"Where are you going?" she demanded.

At the table, he set down the blue folders, one at each of the two chairs. "Come here. Sit down."

She folded her arms protectively across her middle and aimed her chin high. "Not doing it. Just not."

He came toward her again, his blue eyes holding hers, a slight smile curving those sexy lips of his. "Bren."

"I just don't feel right about it, Travis. I really don't."

He took her by the shoulders and dipped his dark head close. "One step at a time. There's no win in just rushing to a negative conclusion."

"I can't help it. Negative is how I feel. I hate this. Hate. It. Am I making myself clear?"

He squeezed her shoulders. "Stop freaking out. We'll

read what it says in the contract and then we'll call Ryan and find out what our options are."

"Wait a minute." She blinked up at him. "You mean Ryan Roarke?"

"Yep."

She had to admit that calling Ryan wasn't a half-bad idea. Ryan was married to Travis's cousin Kristen. The couple lived in Kalispell now, and Ryan had a small practice there. But before he came to Montana, Kristen's husband used to be a lawyer in LA. "I think I heard he was in entertainment law when he lived in California…"

"Exactly. He's an expert on just this sort of thing."

"*If* he's available on zero notice."

"He's a good guy. He'll come right over if he possibly can."

Ryan had experience. A marriage clause in a reality show contract wouldn't be all that shocking to him. Somehow, it didn't seem quite as bad to consider consulting with Ryan as it would be to have to face Travis's dad.

"Dren," Travis said again, so softly. "We really need to run the contracts by a professional, anyway. And Ryan will be bound by attorney-client privilege. He's not telling our secrets to anybody."

"I know that."

"Come here." He pulled her close. She surrendered to his offer of comfort, sliding her arms around his lean waist and laying her cheek against his hard chest. "One step at a time," he whispered and stroked a hand down her hair.

She breathed in his woodsy scent. "Right. Okay. We call Ryan and we ask for his help."

* * *

"My advice, if you sign," said Ryan, "is that you need to be ready to follow through with the on-camera wedding."

Travis glanced at Brenna. She didn't look happy, but at least she seemed calmer now. For a while there he'd been afraid she might run out the door and keep running all the way to the O'Reilly place, taking their chance at *The Great Roundup* along with her.

Brenna said, "What if we sign and then *don't* follow through?"

Ryan lifted a shoulder in a half shrug. "Expect a lawsuit. One you will lose. The terms here are very clear. If Real Deal Entertainment chooses to activate this clause, you're legally bound to do what you agreed to do. You have to marry on the show and then remain legally married until March 31 of next year."

"The final show's airing around Christmas—or I think that's the plan, anyway," Travis said. "So that we have to stay married until spring makes sense, I guess. They would want us married for at least a few months after the whole country gets a front-row seat at our wedding."

Ryan focused on the contract in front of him again and then looked up. "It doesn't require that you live together, though. That means you can essentially go your separate ways as soon as filming wraps."

"That's such a relief," muttered Brenna, clearly meaning it was anything but.

Ryan raked a hank of dark hair off his forehead. It fell right back across his brow. "Just curious. What happens if you tell them you're not willing to sign this clause?"

"Best guess?" asked Brenna. At Ryan's nod, she continued, "There are four of us still to be eliminated from the cast of the show. If we don't sign the marriage clause, Trav and I will be two of the four who have to go."

"But you don't know that for certain. I'm just saying there are unknowns in this equation. Maybe they're bluffing you and they plan to hire one or the other or both of you even if you won't sign on for a wedding. You could bluff back."

Travis glanced across at Brenna. Those sea-blue eyes were waiting. She slowly shook her head. He took her meaning as clearly as if she'd spoken aloud—and he agreed with her, too. If they didn't sign on to be married, this adventure was over.

After Ryan left, Travis suggested, "Let's go downstairs to the Manor Bar. At a time like this, what you need is a big burger and a double order of fries." When she only shook her head again, he came up with a second option. "Or we can call Steve and Roberta, see if they want to hang out for a while."

Brenna sank to the side of her bed. "You go ahead. I need a little time, you know, to think this over."

He wanted to coax her some more, see if he could snap her out of this dark mood of hers. Even if this was the end—and damn it, he hoped not—he hated to see her so down.

"Please," she said. "Just go."

So he left her. He worked out in the basement gym to take some of the tension off. When he came back upstairs, he found a Do Not Disturb sign on her door.

He had a shower and then called Steve. They met up with old Wally Wilson and a couple of other finalists for burgers and fries in the bar. After the meal, they went up to Wally's room and played poker till a little after eleven.

When Travis returned to his room that time, he found the Do Not Disturb sign still hanging on Brenna's door.

Well, all right then. If she wanted to brood all night, fine. He was done trying to cheer the woman up. He left her alone.

After changing into sweats and a T-shirt, he stretched out on the bed and channel surfed for a while. Somehow, he managed to resist the temptation to knock on the door between their rooms. At some point, he must have dropped off to sleep.

He jerked awake to the sound of someone tapping on the interior door.

"Trav?"

He blinked to clear the sleep from his brain. "Brenna?" Was he dreaming?

More tapping. "Travis, can I come in?"

He jumped up so fast he tripped over his boots, which he'd dropped at the side of the bed. A string of curse words escaped him as he grabbed the bedpost, barely keeping himself from landing face-first on the floor.

"Trav?"

"Coming!" Flicking the lock, he hauled back the door. Her side was already open.

She stood there in the same Bushwacker shirt she'd been wearing the morning he took her from her parents' house. Her hair was a wild red tangle around her pale, serious face.

She swallowed hard. And then, out of nowhere, she said, "I got arrested in Juárez."

He tried to think of what to say to that. She looked so fragile right then, like if he touched her she might shatter into a million little pieces and he'd never get her put back together again. He was still trying to figure out how to offer her comfort when she opened her mouth and the story just came spilling out.

"I wasn't even supposed to *be* in Juárez, you know? It was a trip with my girlfriends to El Paso." She rattled off three names he vaguely recognized, girls who had gone to Rust Creek Falls High. None of them lived in town anymore. "It was a reunion trip, me and my girls from back in school. Leonie lives in El Paso now, so we all met up there. We were hanging out, seeing the sights. I fell asleep in the backseat and the next thing I knew, it was dark and Leonie was parking the car not far from this Juárez dive."

He got the picture. "You'd crossed the border while you were sleeping?"

"Exactly. I started to argue that we shouldn't even be there. Marlena said they were going in and I could sit in the car if I wanted to. And I...well, the street was dark and I didn't want to sit there alone. But it was more than that. You know me. We were already there and it was kind of dangerous and exciting..."

He took her sweet face between his two hands. "Hey. It's me, Travis, you're talking to here."

"Oh, Trav..."

"I get it. You don't have to explain. You didn't want to sit out in the car in the dark— and you were curious, so you went in with them."

She held his eyes. "Yeah, I went in. And at first it was fine, not much different than a Friday night at the Ace, just with everyone speaking Spanish and Tejano music on the jukebox. But then it turned out some kind of a drug deal was going down. There was shouting and then shooting. The police showed up and hauled everyone in the place to jail."

He let his hands trail down to her shoulders and then took her arm. "Come on." She let him pull her to the edge of his unmade bed, and she sat when he gently pushed her down. "Were you hurt?"

She shook her head. "We were all okay. Just terrified. They kept us in that jail for three days, in a big holding cell full of desperate-looking women. I got questioned a few times. They were trying to figure out who was in on the drug deal, I think. Finally, they let us make a phone call each. And in the end, my dad and Ronan had to fly down and bail me out. It was awful. I've never seen my dad so disappointed in me. And my mom…she didn't speak to me for weeks. Because, you know, we are O'Reillys. And an O'Reilly doesn't get herself arrested in a Juárez dive bar. That just doesn't happen. After that, I swore off adventure and taking chances. I promised myself and my family that I was settling down."

He put his arm around her and pulled her close to his side. Truth was, he liked how she fit there—maybe too much. "And now here you are, running off with troublesome Travis Dalton to be on a reality show."

"Yeah." She sagged against him, her head tipped down. "You said it." But then she looked up at him. Now those eyes blazed blue fire. "I want it, Trav. I really, really want it. I want to be on *The Great Roundup* with you. I want us to win a million bucks."

He smoothed a hand down her sleep-scrambled hair. It snapped with electricity under his palm. Damn. They were doing this. They were *really* doing this. "I hear you. I get you. I do."

"I want it enough that I'm willing to sign the marriage clause, willing to go through with the wedding if we have to." Her eyes were enormous oceans of blue. "Because if we have to get married, that means we win, right—or at least that we get really close?"

"That's right. That is exactly what it means." But now he felt wary. Now that she knew what she wanted, his conscience had suddenly decided to kick in. He couldn't help wondering if this was the right thing to do.

She saw the change in him. "Uh-uh. Don't you back down now, Travis Dalton. Don't you dare."

"I just want you to be sure, that's all."

"I *am* sure."

"I want it bad, too, but you have to be all in with this. If they make us get married, we'll be going through with it. And then, next spring, we'll be getting a divorce. And not only do O'Reillys *not* get arrested in Juárez dive bars…"

"An O'Reilly does *not* get divorced," she finished for him. "I know it. It's all I've been thinking about all day and all night. And you know what? I still want this. I want to get on that show and I want to win. And that is why we are doing this."

His heart beat a triumphant tattoo under his ribs. "You're certain, then?"

"I'm positive. Tomorrow we tell them we're signing the marriage clause."

At noon the next day, Travis and Brenna signed their contracts.

At three, the final four contestants were eliminated. Brenna and Travis, Steve, Roberta, Wally and Summer Knight all made the cast.

Roger, the field producer, gave a little pep talk, finishing with, "Congratulations to all of you. Relax and rest up tomorrow, get in touch with your loved ones and share your big news. On Monday, you'll all be going on location. And on Tuesday, filming begins."

Rest? Brenna couldn't rest. That night, she did a lot of pillow punching and no sleeping. She couldn't stop second-guessing her choice to sign the marriage clause.

In the morning, she looked bad, with some serious dark circles under her eyes, but she hadn't changed her mind about her ultimate choice. The show would be the experience of a lifetime—and a way to finance her plans for the future.

Also, well, who could say what would happen? Even if she or Travis won, the show's story could change and they wouldn't have to get married, after all. As of now, though, her choice had been made and she was through stewing over it. She showered and dressed and put on more makeup than usual—enough to cover the evidence of her restless night.

Travis, on the other hand, looked fresh and ready for anything when she opened the inner door to him. Apparently, second thoughts hadn't messed with *his* sleep.

He breezed into her room. "I could eat a side of beef. Let's order up some breakfast." He grabbed the room service menu off the table. Really, the man ate like there was no tomorrow and remained lean, his muscles sharply cut, not an ounce of fat on him.

"Where do you put it all, that's what I want to know?"

Travis only chuckled and picked up the phone.

An hour later, their plates were empty. They sat at the table enjoying second cups of coffee, trying to decide how to spend their last day at the Manor.

There was a tap on the door. Assuming it would be Steve or Roberta, Brenna jumped up to answer.

She opened the door to find her sister Fallon on the other side. With a happy cry, she reached for a hug, then stepped back and pulled her baby sister into the room. "It's *so* good to see you. When did you get back from Florida?"

"Yesterday."

"You didn't call."

"I thought I'd surprise you." Fallon spotted Travis. "Hey, Travis."

He got up and hugged her, too. "How was Disney World?"

Fallon, tall and slim as a willow wand, her hair a riot of O'Reilly-red curls and her china-blue eyes shining bright, had never looked happier. "The kids ran us ragged." The triplets were just fourteen months old. "We loved every minute of it." She gave Trav a radiant smile that wavered a little when she added, "I understand congratulations are in order."

"Thanks." Travis played his part so perfectly. He reached out a hand and Brenna went to him, tucking herself up close to his side as though she was born to be there. And truthfully, sometimes she could almost believe that he actually did love her, that they were finally *really* together and nothing could ever drag them apart. He pressed a kiss to her temple, his lips so warm and soft. "I snagged the pot of gold with this one, that's for sure—and I'll get out of here and let you two catch up."

"It's good to see you, Travis," said Fallon as he turned for the inside door to his room.

He paused in the doorway. "You, too. You look great,

Fallon. I can see that married life is working for you. My best to Jamie."

"I'll tell him you said hi."

With a last nod, Travis went into his room, pulling the door shut behind him.

"Coffee?" Brenna offered. "There's some in the carafe."

"Sounds perfect."

Brenna got her sister a clean cup and they sat down together. "There's toast," she offered. "And blackberry jam."

"Just the coffee." Fallon took the cup Brenna handed her and raised it toward the door to Travis's room. "He's such a charmer."

"Always and forever," Brenna agreed.

"Mom told me a cute story. You know Abby Fuller?"

"Yeah, Marissa Fuller's nine-year-old." Marissa was widowed with three girls. Abby was the oldest.

"Abby's adorable," said Fallon. "All three of those little girls are. Anyway, Marissa told Mom that Abby thinks Travis is dreamy—Abby's word, I kid you not. Abby says she's going to marry herself a cowboy someday…if she can't marry the lead singer of 2LOVEU." The sisters laughed together. "Remind you of anyone?"

"Oh, yeah. Brings back precious memories." She saw herself at six, when Travis brought her bike back after Angus McCauley stole it. "I planned to marry a cowboy, too."

"A certain cowboy."

"Yep."

"And just look at you now."

"That's right." Fake engaged to be legally married—and divorced come the spring.

Fallon frowned. "What's wrong?"

"Are you kidding? Not a thing."

Fallon sipped her coffee. "Downstairs, I asked for you at the front desk. A short guy with a big smile appeared."

"Gerry, the production assistant."

"He was sweet. He said he could have guessed that we were sisters and of course I could see you. He gave me your room number." She set down her cup. "So. Lots going on with you, huh? *The Great Roundup*, for real?"

Brenna shared her news. "We found out yesterday that we made the final cut. We go on location tomorrow."

"Oh, my gosh. Seriously?"

"That's right. We're in. It's a big step —but also just the beginning. We've got six weeks of filming to get through."

"You have to tell me everything as soon as you get back."

"Sorry, can't do that." She explained about the confidentiality agreement.

"That's no fair. Your own sister has to wait to find out what happened?"

"You know if I could tell anyone, it would be you." Brenna wanted to grab her and hug her all over again. "Oh, Fallon. It's so good to see you."

"You are amazing," her sister said. "I admit I've envied the way you throw yourself into life. You've always been ready for anything. I used to wish that I could be as brave as you."

Brenna got misty-eyed. She sniffed. "Don't you dare make me cry— and I noticed you said 'used to wish.'"

"Well, as it so happens, my life is turning out to be

pretty amazing, too." Fallon had loved Jamie Stockton all her life. And now she was married to him. "I'm so happy, Bren. I can't tell you."

"I'm glad."

Fallon reached across the table. Her soft fingers brushed Brenna's. "Just…be careful, okay?"

Brenna tried to keep it light. "Me? Careful? Never gonna happen."

"I think Travis is a great guy, you know that. And he seems really crazy about you…"

"But…?" Brenna drew out the word.

"I know you've had a thing for him for years. And I'm glad it's working out for you two. But, well…"

Brenna couldn't stand it. "Look. I know what you're going to say. He's thirty-four and I'm his first serious relationship." *Or I would be, if it wasn't all just for the show.* "Not to mention, he's got that rep as a player, right?"

"I'm your sister. It's my job to say the hard stuff— or in this case, to make *you* say it." Fallon gave a weak laugh.

"Well, okay then. You've done your part. And please don't worry about me. I can handle myself, and I know what I'm doing. *The Great Roundup* is a once-in-a-life-time opportunity, and there is no way I'm passing it up."

Fallon stood. She stepped around the table to Brenna's side.

Brenna looked at her sister. "What?"

Fallon pulled her to her feet and looked directly into her eyes. "Bren, what is really going on here?"

Brenna lied without flinching. "I don't know what you're talking about."

"Oh, honey." Fallon stroked her hand down Brenna's

hair. "I notice you haven't told me how much you love him."

Okay, so she'd blown it. At the moment, she felt crappy enough about the whole thing that she didn't even care. She straightened her shoulders. "That Friday night at the Ace, the night he asked me to marry him? That night I said it a lot of times. You can ask anyone."

"But you're not saying it now, to me. Is this whole engagement thing just a stunt to get you on the show?"

Brenna didn't answer. She hated lying to her sister. And right now, she just wasn't going to do it. Let Fallon think what she wanted.

"You're not answering me," Fallon accused softly. When Brenna still said nothing, Fallon grabbed her in a tight hug. "Bren, please just be careful," she whispered. "Be careful and try not to get hurt."

Chapter Six

At six on Monday morning, Gerry tapped on Brenna's door.

"Top o' the mornin' to ye, Brenna, m' love. I need to see your suitcases and go through all the drawers in your room."

"Uh. Because?"

"My darling, some items are not allowed on location. If you have any of those, they'll be boxed up for you and available as soon as filming wraps."

"Items such as…?"

"Ropes, tack, compasses, fire starters, anything you might use in a challenge. All contestants use the equipment provided on-site. Weapons, drugs, narcotics. Video games, iPods. Medications you didn't get approved ahead of time. The list goes on."

"What about my phone?"

"You can bring it on location, but you'll turn it in there. We'll keep it charged for you and return it to you for approved phone calls and other special circumstances—and just FYI, it's all in the contract, my sweet."

She vaguely remembered all that. "All righty, then." She let him in and he went through all the drawers, both of her suitcases and her makeup kit, too, confiscating a bottle of aspirin, her old iPod and her iPad. He bagged and labeled them, stuck them in the pack he had with him and then went and knocked on Travis's door.

Once she was packed, dressed and ready to go, Travis joined her in her room and they ordered up some breakfast.

As they ate, they went over the series of simple signals they'd worked out. A tug on the left ear meant one thing, on the right, another. On set, they would be wearing body mics. Anything they said would be recorded, so they needed ways to communicate without words until they could steal a little privacy for a real conversation.

Their signals memorized, they left their rooms for the last time.

"This is it," Travis warned. "From now on, assume we're being filmed and recorded at all times. We're madly in love and engaged to be married. Play that for all you're worth and don't say or do anything to give our game away."

She clutched his arm and gazed up at him adoringly. "I love you with every fiber of my being and I can't wait to be your wife."

He gave a nod of approval. "Sell it, Bren."

"Oh, just you watch me."

* * *

Downstairs, they loaded their gear into a large, no-frills white van and Gerry drove them and half the contestants the twenty-five miles to High Lonesome Guest Ranch. The other half of the cast followed an hour later in an identical van. The whole idea, Gerry said, was to transport the contestants without drawing attention to them and giving away their supersecret shooting location.

In a rolling valley surrounded by mountains blanketed in thick evergreen, the ranch had been leased to Real Deal for the duration of filming. Gerry said the owners were in the process of converting the place from a working ranch to a guest facility. They were still building guest cottages and doing finish work on various interiors and wouldn't open for business until next spring. Real Deal had gotten an excellent rate for the exclusive use of the property during filming, and High Lonesome would reap the benefit of all that free publicity for its opening season.

It was a beautiful site, acres and acres of gorgeous land, all those tall trees with a few craggy, snow-capped, cloud-ringed peaks looming in the distance. There were stables, two barns and a series of linked corrals and paddocks. Green pastures dotted with patches of bright wildflowers were home to a herd of grazing cattle. Besides a number of cozy log cottages, the property boasted a fancy main lodge.

Inside the lodge they got their room assignments. Again, Brenna and Travis ended up side by side with a connecting door.

Summer Knight had the room on Travis's other side, so they rode up in the elevator together. Summer dimpled and fluttered her eyelashes at Travis, the way she'd done every chance she got during their stay at the Manor. Brenna tried not to be too aggravated with the woman. Summer flirted with all the guys, even old Wally Wilson and the seventeen-year-old Franklin twins, Rob and Joey, who had joined the cast with their father, Fred.

"Don't let her get you alone," she teased Travis a few minutes later, after they'd dropped their bags on their beds and opened the adjoining door. "She might try anything."

He moved in close. "Jealous?"

She was, just a little. And that annoyed her almost as much as Summer did. "Let Summer put a move on you and you'll find out."

He actually smirked. "You can't fool me. You're jealous. I kind of like that."

Saying she wasn't would only serve to convince him that she was. So she rolled with it. "As your adoring fiancée, it's my job to act jealous—of Summer, especially."

"Why Summer?"

"She's a man-eater."

"And you know this how?"

"Oh, please. Take my word for it. And stay away from her."

"Or...?"

"Really? Seriously? You're doubling down?"

Now he put on his wounded face. "Oh, come on. You know I was only kidding."

"I do?"

"As your husband-to-be, I would never even look at another woman."

"Travis. Get real. You were pretty much born to flirt."

He faked a look of pure longing. "Not since you stole my heart."

She pantomimed gagging with her hands to her throat as the phone by the bed rang. He picked it up. "We'll be right down," he said and hung up. "They want us in the lobby—and we have to bring our phones."

Downstairs, production assistants bagged and tagged their cell phones. Then Anthony Locke and Roger Del-Ray welcomed them all to High Lonesome and introduced them to the show's host, Jasper Ridge, who would narrate the various challenges and run the eliminations.

Jasper clearly had a thing for black. He looked like some old-time bad guy, in black jeans, a black shirt, a black bandanna and a black hat. When he tipped his hat, the hair underneath was patent-leather black, too. He had actual sideburns and a black handlebar mustache.

"Enjoy today and tonight at the lodge. But remember," Roger warned them all, "*The Great Roundup* is not a luxury vacation. Starting tomorrow, you'll be living outside—mic'd up and on camera twelve to eighteen hours a day." He introduced some of the crew, including the story editor, associate directors and various assistants.

"Hospitality services will keep a buffet available until ten tonight in the dining room." Roger pointed toward a hallway. "Through there. Spend the day getting acquainted with the property. Check out the canteen. Ride the horses if you want to. Stable grooms are there to help you. Everyone take a backpack." He indicated the stacks of them on a long table against an interior wall. "Fill them with the basics in clothing and toiletries. Just what will fit in the packs. Everything else you'll turn in to the concierge desk before call time tomorrow."

A couple of assistants passed out call sheets that showed who had to be where at which times for the next day's work. A glance at her copy told Brenna they were mostly for the crew, who had a somewhat staggered schedule. For the cast, it was pretty much show up in the lobby at 5:00 a.m. armed with your full pack and ready to roll.

After they were dismissed and they stowed their backpacks upstairs, Brenna and Travis took a tour of the ranch with Steve and Roberta.

They checked out the available horses, looked over the equipment in the tack room and visited the canteen, a glorified tent set up out of sight of the lodge. Inside the canteen, long tables were piled with foodstuffs, cooking utensils, a few basic tools and various outdoor gear, including tents and camping stuff.

After lunch, they chose horses, tacked them up and rode out to get a better look at the property.

Brenna was impressed by Steve's abilities. Though he'd lost his left leg below the knee and wore a prosthesis, she'd never guess it to see him on a horse. He'd been raised on a West Texas cattle ranch, where his dad, stepmom and three little half brothers still lived.

When Brenna complimented his riding skill, Steve flashed his gorgeous smile. "Six weeks out from my last surgery, soon as I got my doctor's approval, I moved back to the ranch and started riding again."

Roberta knew her way around a horse, too. She might have been living in the city for the past twenty years, but she'd grown up on a horse ranch near Santa Barbara.

Brenna realized they'd both present some serious competition.

It was past six when they returned to the stables. They took care of their horses and went in to eat.

Later that evening, Wally Wilson got out his battered old guitar—the rules allowed musical instruments as long as they weren't amplified or electronic. The old man sat by the big stone fireplace in the lodge's great room and played country songs that had been popular back when Brenna's folks were kids.

It was nice, kind of homey, with everyone gathered around the fire. Some knew the words to the old songs and sang along.

Travis led Brenna to a club chair by the window. Brenna played her part, sitting crossways on his lap, letting her boots dangle over the chair arm. She rested her cheek against his shoulder. As he idly stroked her hair, she settled in with a contented sigh and decided that reality TV wasn't bad, really. Not bad at all.

There were no cameras that she noticed at first, but Anthony Locke and his minions must have seen the opportunity and grabbed it. She looked over and spotted a cameraman in one corner and a guy with a boom mic homing in on old Wally. And now that she was paying attention, she noticed the cameras mounted in the rafters.

She must have stiffened, because Trav leaned down to kiss the top of her head and asked, "What is it?"

She snuggled her face into his neck and pretended to kiss him there. He smelled so good, of leather and man. "Cameras," she whispered. "Everywhere."

He chuckled as though she'd said something really amusing. "Get used to it," he whispered back.

"It's creepy."

He tipped up her chin. They shared a long look. Oh, really, she could pretend to be Travis's girl for the rest of her life, easy-peasy. He kissed her, his warm lips so soft, his beard thrillingly scratchy. "Embrace the creepy."

"More reality show wisdom?"

"You said it."

"Next you'll be reminding me that I signed on for this."

Travis said nothing. He just kissed her again.

"Get a room!" one of the Franklin boys heckled. Somebody else snickered.

Brenna smiled to herself as she settled her head back on Travis's shoulder. If she had to play a bride-to-be who couldn't keep her hands off her man, at least she got to do it with the best kisser in Montana.

At five the next morning, they all gathered downstairs in the lobby to get their body mics. The mics came in two pieces connected by a wire—a microphone, which you hooked to your shirt or pinned in your hair, and a transmitter, which went in a pocket. The mics could record a whisper at three feet away. Contestants were expected to wear them throughout the working day.

Before they went outside, Roger introduced the wranglers— crew members who wrangled the cast. Dressed in jeans, boots and dark shirts, the wranglers would help to keep track of who was doing what and where, all while keeping themselves mostly invisible. They wore headsets to get instructions from Roger, Anthony and the story editors. They would also consult off camera with the judges when it came time to determine winners and losers.

Hospitality served them all breakfast outside at picnic tables. And then, as the sun came up, with the cameras rolling, Anthony had the contestants grouped at the entrance to the canteen. Brenna, next to Travis, played her part for the camera, holding his arm, glancing up at him adoringly, staying in good and close.

Jasper emerged from within and started talking. It was an intro to the show. For the benefit of the TV audience, Jasper explained the rules that all of the contestants had already read and agreed to. There were to be major challenges and minor ones. If you won a minor challenge, you got some small perk. If you won a major challenge, you got immunity from elimination in the next round.

And if you didn't have immunity and the judges gave you the lowest score on a major challenge? Bye-bye.

Jasper introduced the judges, three old cowpunchers, each with a hat bigger than the one before. The one with the biggest hat explained in a lazy drawl that points would be given for skill, daring, teamwork and the successful accomplishment of each major challenge. The points didn't accumulate. Once the judging of any given challenge was over, everyone still in the game started fresh. All you had to do was survive each major challenge to remain in the running.

As Jasper talked, the wranglers ran around whispering directions in people's ears. Apparently, one of them told Summer Knight to cozy up to Travis, because the rodeo star popped up out of nowhere on Trav's other side.

Like a shark gliding through deep water, the woman

had gotten to him without a sound. Brenna sensed movement in her peripheral vision. When she glanced around Travis, there was Summer, up close and personal, flashing him a big, flirty smile.

Brenna considered not reacting. But then the whole point was the drama, right? Where was the drama if she just let it go?

She grabbed Travis's hand.

"What?" he whispered, which was a total crock on every level. He knew exactly what. And his whisper might not disturb Jasper's endless monologue, but their body mics picked up every slight sound they made. Brenna just shook her head and dragged him around Fred Franklin and the twins to the far edge of the group.

When she stopped, Travis pulled his hand free of her grip—but only so he could slide his arm around her neck and pull her in close. He kissed her cheek, a sweet little peck that she enjoyed way too much. "'Fess up, baby," he said softly in a country twang. "You're jealous. You know you are. But you don't need to be. 'Cause, darlin', all I see is you."

Sheesh. He should put that line to music.

She almost laughed but caught herself and put on a sulky little glare instead.

Objectively, she got that this was just what the director had been going for. Jasper was a pretty good talker. He made all that information as interesting as possible. But come on, listening to rules and instructions was a snooze. A little drama on the side would liven things up.

She was just starting to feel smug that she'd thwarted the man-eater. But no. Here came Summer again, slipping into position on Travis's other side. They ought to play the theme music from *Jaws* wherever that woman went. Summer flashed a radiant smile—first at Brenna and then right at Travis.

Brenna simply couldn't let that move stand. She had her pride, after all.

She ducked free of Travis's hold and slid around to his other side. "'Scuse me," she whispered, all innocence, and eased herself between her fake fiancé and the man-stealing rodeo star.

Summer only sighed and turned her eyes front, suddenly totally enthralled as Jasper described their first task on the show: they would each be creating their own immunity bracelet. After each major challenge, the winner would put on his or her bracelet, thus acquiring immunity from elimination during the next major challenge.

They got to work braiding bracelets out of strips of leather using colored beads for decoration. Brenna was pretty good at it. She and Fallon had played around with making leather bracelets back in their teens. Plus, as a hairdresser, Brenna knew how to get a tight, even braid. She added purple and turquoise beads in various shapes and sizes to jazz her bracelet up a little and had it finished in no time.

Trav was another story. Judging by his lumpy-looking effort, crafting with leather wasn't something he'd ever tried. He got a look at Brenna's bracelet and gave her the sexy eyes. "Gee, Bren. How 'bout helping me out a little here?"

She showed him how to hold the leather strings with even tension and suggested he use azure-blue beads. "Because they match your eyes."

He gave her that smile that could melt panties at

fifty paces and leaned in for a quick kiss that some-how stretched out into something longer. And deeper.

Seriously, forget bracelet making. Maybe she and Trav could stand here kissing for the next hour or two. They could call the show *The Great Romance Roundup*. And forget the ranching challenges. It could be all about kissing and togetherness, about deep, meaningful shar-ing and beautiful declarations of undying love.

Was it wrong to feel this good when she was kissing him? His lips played over hers. She reached up a hand and stroked the hair at his temple. He pulled her closer into the circle of his lean arms.

About then, though, it started to seem way too quiet around them. Brenna broke the kiss and opened her eyes to find everybody watching and more than one camera aimed at them.

Trav seemed to shake himself. "Bracelets, right? We're making bracelets…"

She laughed and took his bracelet from him. "Okay, pay attention, now."

He caught on quickly. Roberta signaled Brenna. Brenna went to give her a hand.

An hour later, she'd helped seven other contestants make their bracelets. Wally Wilson had some experi-ence with leatherwork, too. He'd taken Brenna's lead and pitched in to give pointers to anyone having trouble.

Wally ended up helping Summer, who shamelessly flirted with him the whole time. Actually, it was kind of cute watching Wally flirt back. He had that cowboy way about him, both shy and courtly at the same time.

As soon as everyone had completed a bracelet, Jas-per emerged from the canteen carrying a large, shallow wooden box intricately carved with Western scenes. He raised the lid to reveal twenty-two labeled slots, one for each contestant. One by one, he called them forward to lay their bracelets in the box.

It was all very solemn and ceremonious. And when the box was filled, Jasper closed the lid and handed it off to one of the wranglers, who disappeared with it back into the canteen.

"Next task," announced Jasper. "Set up camp."

Jasper made a big show of inviting them into the canteen, where the piles of equipment had been arranged on the tables and labeled with their names, one for each cast member. The married couple, Leah and Seth Stone, had one pile labeled with both their names. So did Travis and Brenna.

That was when it hit her. They were sharing a tent.

When Brenna turned those turquoise blue eyes on him, Travis expected her to look freaked. But in fact, on the surface, she seemed fine with the tent arrangements.

And why wouldn't she be? They were lovers, after all, and engaged to be married. Of course they would want to be sleeping together.

But Travis knew she didn't like it. It was one thing to have adjoining rooms with a door to shut between them. But it was another altogether to sleep side by side every night in the close confines of a tent.

Because in real life they simply weren't *that* intimate.

He wrapped an arm around her waist, hauled her close and nuzzled her ear. "We got lucky, darlin'," he whispered, for the benefit of their body mics.

And they *had* gotten lucky, at least in terms of the tent itself. He'd expected they would have to sleep out in the open. A tent was a bonus.

But Brenna still seemed too subdued when he let her go, so the next time she glanced his way, he tugged on his left ear, their signal for *Let's talk as soon as possible.*

Actually the talk signal was intended for emergencies, when one of them had some urgent bit of info to communicate to the other. But he didn't have a signal for *Please don't freak out. I'll explain why the shared tent is a good thing as soon as we're alone.* So he worked with what he had.

"Gotcha," she said. He took that to mean she'd understood the signal. They grabbed their gear.

The tents went up in a wide circle on a large, mostly cleared space a quarter mile from the canteen. Furnishings were minimal: bedrolls, sleeping bags, their packs and a battery-powered lantern for each tent. Each contestant had a camp chair to call their own.

Once the shelters were up and ready, they all pitched in together to build the community campfire in the center of their little tent village. Like putting up a tent, building a campfire was a basic skill for all of them. They worked together smoothly, everybody pitching in. There were a few slackers, especially Dean Fogarth, a sandy-haired cowboy in his early twenties who spent a lot of time trying to impress Summer. But the job wasn't big enough or difficult enough for anyone to care much if Dean didn't do his part.

Wally and a couple of the other guys prepped the flat, open spot in the center of the tent circle. They cleared away debris and brought buckets of gravel up from the side of the nearby creek for better drainage when it rained and to keep the heat from sterilizing the ground beneath the blaze. Most of the women, Brenna included, began gathering firewood.

Travis helped by hauling rocks to make the fire ring. Through a cluster of trees out of sight of the camp, he found a nice stash of granite boulders at the base of a rock slide. He was hefting the first one to carry back to the campsite when Brenna popped out from behind a cottonwood.

He almost dropped the rock on his foot. "What the—"

She signaled frantically for silence and then waved her hand for him to follow her. He put down the rock and trailed her deeper into the grove of trees. When she stopped, she unclipped her mic from her hair, tugged it out from under her shirt and put it in her back pocket. She gestured for him to do the same.

A quick glance around showed no cameramen, no cast members and zero wranglers. Moving the microphone to a pocket would probably mute the sound enough that they wouldn't be heard if they whispered. And as the mic would still be operating, it would take the sound techs a while to realize that something wasn't right.

Travis stashed his mic. "What?" he whispered, in a hurry to know what was so all-fired important she needed to tell him right now.

She blinked. "What do you mean, what? You signaled that you had something to tell me that couldn't wait."

He winced. "Sorry, I just wanted to reassure you."

"Reassure me of what?"

"That there's an upside to sharing a tent. If we keep it low, we'll probably be able to talk every night—you know, make plans. Strategize."

She looked at him the way his mom used to, back when he was little and did something only a wild-ass, irresponsible kid would do. "You pulled your left ear. That means you've got something you *have* to tell me ASAP."

"Uh…"

"Travis Dalton." She puffed out her cheeks with a hard breath. "There's no emergency, is there?"

"I thought you were upset."

Her expression softened. "Well, that's kind of sweet— and honestly, I'm okay."

"Sure?"

"Positive."

He suggested, "Because we could tell them we need separate tents, that sex before marriage is against our beliefs."

She burst out laughing —and then clapped her hand over her mouth to keep too much sound from escaping. Finally, she whispered, "The way we've been going at each other? No one's going to believe we're a couple of innocent virgins. And even if we were, well, there's no reason we couldn't share a tent and keep our hands to ourselves. I mean, in the old days, engaged people used to share the same bed. It was called bundling. They would put a board between them so that—"

"Stop. I know what bundling is. And no board is going to keep two sex-starved kids apart."

"They had integrity back then."

"And a bunch of unplanned pregnancies, I'll bet. You should start worrying."

"About?"

"You're so hot," he teased, just to watch her cheeks turn pink. "What if I can't control myself?"

She did blush—just a little. And then she scowled to cover it. "Save the shameless flattery for the cameras." She reached out and grabbed him by the shirtfront, yanking him close. "And don't mess with the signals."

She was one hundred percent dead-on right about that. They couldn't afford to risk pissing off the powers that be over nothing. And she was really cute when she was mad. "Yes, ma'am." Her skin had the sweetest flush on it. He admired the pale freckles scattered across the delicate bridge of her nose. "And come to think of it, there's a good chance they've mounted a camera in these trees somewhere. Don't look around. You'll give us away."

She stiffened and kept her eyes locked with his. "Fine." He bent a little closer. "What are you up to?" Her whisper sizzled with suspicion.

"Ask yourself, what do lovers do when they manage to steal a moment alone?"

And then she smiled. "Got it." She lifted her head up that extra inch so their lips could meet.

Yeah.

Kissing Bren. He was getting way too used to it. And it felt too damn good, dangerously so.

But he'd never been the kind of guy to let a little danger stop him. He had a part to play, after all. He ran his tongue along the sweet seam where her soft lips touched. With a sigh, she let him in.

He took shameless advantage, tasting her deeply. She sighed again, like she couldn't get enough.

Really, they were so good at this kissing thing. Too good. More and more lately, he forgot that she was still little Brenna O'Reilly and he'd always vowed never to make a move on her. Somehow, the longer they pretended to be crazy in love, the harder it got to stop his mind from spinning fantasies about what it might be like, the two of them, together. For real.

He imagined taking it further, maybe letting his hand slide up from where he clasped her waist—up over the slim shape of her beneath her soft plaid shirt, up and up, until he cupped her breast. He would tease her nipple with his thumb until it got hard and tight and he could feel it even through her bra.

Damn. He really needed to dial it back. He was getting excited—and she knew it, too. A sharp gasp escaped her. For one delicious second, she surged even closer, pressing her hips to the growing hardness at his fly.

And then she yanked those soft hips away. Breaking the kiss, she stared up at him. He tried to force an easy grin when all he really wanted was to pull her back good and close, cover those fine lips again and kiss her some more.

He would kiss her all over, take her down to the mossy ground under the cottonwoods and not let her up until he'd had a real taste, a deeper taste. A taste that included every smooth, pretty inch of her.

Still staring wide-eyed, she let go of his shirt. Her breathing was agitated. But she was still Bren. In a split second, she pulled it together, giving him a crooked grin and advising, "I think you'd better pull your mic out of your pocket now and get back to hauling boulders."

A couple of hours later, the community campfire had a ring of boulders all the way around and a fire laid, tepee-style, all ready to go. Wally did the honors, striking a storm-proof match from the boxes that had been provided in their piles of equipment. The dried leaves inside the tepee of sticks caught fire.

Dinner was canned chili, which they heated over the fire along with mini hot dogs, also from a can. Real Deal provided all the water anyone could drink, offered in ten-gallon watercoolers. For cleanup, they carried their pots and plates to the creek down a gentle slope west of the campsite. And when nature called, a pair of porta-potties rigged up to look like old-time outhouses waited on the far side of the stream.

After dinner, they relaxed by the campfire. But the day's work wasn't done. One by one, they were called for OTFs—individual on-the-fly interviews.

"You pulled Travis away from Summer this morning outside the canteen when she moved in close to him," Roger said to Brenna when it was her turn. "And then, when she followed you and Travis to the edge of the group, you got between her and your fiancé. Why?"

It was after nine at night. Brenna sat in a camp chair just outside the canteen. The camera was on her. Roger was a disembodied voice beyond the circle of light.

Behind her they'd set up what they called a green screen so they could digitally add the background later. They'd lit the night around her in a sort of golden glow, and she assumed that if any of this interview made the show, she would appear to be sitting in front of a campfire.

"Summer's a big flirt," she said. "If she comes after my man, she'll be dealing with me."

"Is that what you were doing this morning?"

She nodded. "That is exactly what I was doing."

"You seemed real calm, real purposeful, when Summer moved in on Travis, but how were you feeling inside?"

"When Summer put her move on Travis at the canteen this morning, I tried to keep a smile on my face, but inside I was angry."

"Do you have a message for Summer?"

"I do." Brenna looked directly into the camera and played her part for all she was worth. "Watch yourself, Summer. Nobody likes a man-stealing tease."

Travis ducked into their darkened tent. "Alone at last," he whispered.

"Find any recording equipment?" she asked. He'd gone out to pee—and to check the perimeter for hidden recording devices. They'd already painstakingly checked their packs, the tent, their sleeping bags and bedrolls and the lantern as well, and found nothing. But you just never knew.

"I couldn't find anything suspicious nearby," he said. "But we should keep it down, just in case." He closed the tent flaps and got into his sleeping bag next to her. Only then did he take off his clothes, pulling each item out of the sleeping bag as he removed it.

Surprisingly, it was fine, cozy. Just her and Travis, finally able to whisper what was on their minds at the end of the day. She couldn't believe that the idea of sharing a tent with him had made her nervous at first. She didn't feel the least bit edgy now. There was nothing to be nervous about—not as long as she didn't let herself dwell on that smoking-hot kiss he'd given her that afternoon.

"I would kill for a bath about now." She pulled a hank of hair in front of her nose. "I smell like a campfire."

He chuckled, the sound low and rich in the darkness. "They've got some sort of outdoor shower setup by one of the barns, so eventually we'll get a turn at those. But still, you need to get used to that grubby feeling. It's only going to get worse."

"Where are the makeup people and hairdressers when a girl needs them?"

"You wear your own clothes and do your own makeup. That's why they call it reality TV."

"Yeah, well. As for makeup, I was lucky to fit blusher, mascara and lip gloss in my pack. But my hair…" Late in the afternoon, the wind had come up and a light rain had fallen. Her hair was no longer smooth and straight. "Ugh. I have no words."

"Your curls came back. I like 'em." She felt his hand on her head, a light caress and then gone. "Springy."

Warmth slid through her at his touch. And not only his touch. Sometimes he said the sweetest things. "I'm braiding it tomorrow. In fact…" She sat up and reached for her pack.

"What are you up to now?"

"I'd better braid it now or it will be nothing but tangles by the morning."

"In the dark?"

"Piece of cake." She felt for her comb, brush and a hair elastic and began brushing it in sections, working out the snarls.

He shifted in his sleeping bag, rolling over to his back. She could see him well enough to watch him put his hands behind his head. "What do you think about Roberta and Steve?"

She switched to her comb to ease out a bad tangle. "I have to say, the way she looks at him…"

A low chuckle from Trav. "And the way *he* looks at *her*. Pow. That's attraction."

Though he probably couldn't see her do it, Brenna shook her head. "Roberta's divorce just became final. It was really bad, she said. That bastard destroyed her. She loved him, and he just traded her in like a car with too many miles on it. She told me she's swearing off men forever."

"But Steve's a great guy."

"Trav, get real. She lives in California, he lives in Texas. She's forty-five, he's thirty. And didn't I just tell you she's swearing off men forever?"

"Some barriers are just made to be broken."

She winced as she forced her comb through another tangle. Really, maybe Travis was right. Up to a point, anyway. "Hmm. Well, on second thought, maybe a fling would be good for both of them."

"Good for their game, too." Meaning their story within the show.

To succeed on a reality show, you not only had to come out ahead in the challenges, you needed a strong emotional game so viewers would root for you. Or love to hate you. After all, good drama needed bad guys as well as good ones.

Travis added way too casually, "And speaking of the game, Summer came after me again while I was hauling rocks."

Brenna felt a little stab of something unpleasant—a certain tightness in her belly. She refused to call it jealousy. "Before or after you and I talked alone?"

"After."

Brenna started braiding swiftly, tugging the sections

of her hair harder than she needed to, hard enough that it hurt a little. "Came after you how?"

"I was working a boulder free of the rock slide. She came up behind me and slapped my ass."

"What in the— You're kidding."

"Nope. When I told her to knock it off, she laughed and took hold of my arm. Caught me off balance and I ended up practically falling on top of her. I grabbed her to steady her..."

The silence in the tent seemed to echo. Outside, very distinctly, Brenna heard the lonely hoot of an owl. She prompted, "And?"

He made a slight throat-clearing sound. "Brenna, you know that it's the story that counts and it's our job to play it and play it good. That's all she's doing, playing her part."

"And what are *you* doing, Trav?" She slipped the hair elastic off her wrist and wrapped it three times around the end of her braid, giving it a final snap for good measure.

"Bren—"

"That was wrong, what she did, slapping you like that. Why are you defending her?" She shoved her comb and brush back into her pack.

"Why are *you* so pissed off all of a sudden?" he demanded. Unfortunately, it was a very good question. One she wasn't going answer—not even to herself. He added, "All I care about is keeping us strong in the game."

The game. Right this minute, she hated the damn game. And that was kind of scary, given that this whole thing was a game—one that she really did want to win, one that had only just begun.

"I'm going to ask you one more time, Travis. You grabbed her to steady her. What happened next?"

Another silence. Somewhere out in the night, that lonely owl hooted.

"She kind of…toppled against me."

"She toppled?"

"Yeah."

"And then?"

"And then, out of nowhere, she grabbed me around the neck and smashed her mouth on mine."

Chapter Seven

"You kissed her," Bren accused in a tiny whisper.

Travis felt like the run-down heel on an old, dirty boot—disreputable and in need of immediate replacement. Kissing Summer had been nothing like kissing Bren. With Bren, he was sorely tempted. With Summer, it was…a calculated transaction. Part of the game.

He opened his mouth to say that of course he hadn't kissed the woman. She'd kissed *him*, and he'd pulled away immediately. "I…" The lie got stuck in his throat, and the truth just slid around it and escaped. "I hesitated. I didn't kiss her back, but for a second or two, when she jumped at me, I didn't push her away, either."

"Why not?" Her whisper was soft, carefully controlled. But she wasn't happy with him. Her disappointment had weight that dragged on his heart. "Are you going to throw me over for Summer, Trav? Is that your game now?"

"Of course not—but yeah, I *was* thinking of the game. I was running through my options. Trying to decide what the best move would be. To let it go on a moment for the drama, or to push her away fast and remind her that I'm engaged."

"Oh, great." Meaning it seriously wasn't. "Now I get to play the jilted fiancée. Everybody back home can watch you mess me over on network TV." She zipped her pack, the sound sharp and furious.

"Of course I'm not jilting you. My alliance is with you."

"Coulda fooled me."

"You're overreacting."

"Oh, I don't think so. I think it's crap what you did, Trav. I think playing Summer's game is the cheap way to go." That hurt. It hurt bad. And she wasn't done yet. "We're supposed to be partners."

"We *are* partners."

"And yet you think it's a good idea to run around behind my back with another woman."

"What are you talking about? It was a couple of seconds with her mouth on mine. Nobody was running around. And I'm *telling* you what happened. How is that behind your back?"

"What about our *Great Roundup* wedding? Does the *game* require that I marry a cheater in front of the world?"

"Of course not."

"If you say 'of course not' one more time, I'm going to scream."

He had the most terrible feeling—that he was losing her. Which made no sense. He'd never even *had* her, and he never would.

"Bren, I swear to you, it was just a split second that I let her kiss me, and then I took her by the shoulders and pushed her away. I told her to back off, that I was engaged and in love with my fiancée and she should try looking for a guy who might actually be interested."

A full ten seconds passed as she absorbed that information. "At least you said that," she gave out grudgingly at last. "Finally."

"I'm not messing around on you, Bren. I would never do that."

"Oh, come on. You've spent your whole life messing around."

Now he was the one letting the silence stretch out. What she said was the truth, as far as it went. So why did it wound him to hear her whispering it at him in the dark?

He answered her honestly. "Well, I think that depends on your definition of messing around. Have I spent time with a lot of different women? Yes. Have I ever cheated? Never. And I never tried to make time with somebody else's girl. I may be the troublesome Dalton who never settled down, but I *am* a Dalton, and a Dalton doesn't cheat."

She didn't say anything. Not for a really long time. Instead, she slid down into her sleeping bag and settled on her side with a long sigh. At least she was facing him. He decided to take that as a good sign.

Then she asked, her whisper softer than ever, "What did Summer do next?"

He didn't want to tell her. But he'd stuck to the painful truth so far. It seemed pretty pointless to start lying now. "She said she'd be waiting when I changed my mind. And then she picked up the armful of sticks she'd gathered and headed for camp."

"I can think of several unattractive names to call Summer Knight."

"It's the game they handed her. She plays it or she's out."

"If I were her, I would come up with a *better* game."

"I have no doubt." He wanted to reach over, brush her shoulder, stroke her hair. But right now, he didn't dare. He kept his hands to himself.

"Trav?"

"Hmm?"

"Did Roger pull you out for an OTF after Summer kissed you?"

"Yeah."

"What did you say?"

"I said that *she* had come after *me*, that it shocked the hell out of me when she kissed me, that I had zero interest in Summer Knight, that I had never led her on and never would. And that you were the only woman for me."

He seemed to have trouble breathing until she finally spoke. "Well, all right." And then she said, "If you do change your mind about how you want to play things—"

"I won't." He said it louder than he should have. And he meant it, absolutely.

"I was only going to say that I would really appreciate it if you'd let me know first."

"You're right. We're a team. I screwed up and I'm sorry. She kissed me and I started calculating options— but I swear all I did was hesitate. I didn't kiss her back."

"She'll consider your hesitation proof that she's making headway with you."

"She's not."

"Be prepared for her to come after you again."

"Next time—if there *is* a next time—she won't catch me off guard. And I *won't* hesitate. I'll tell her to get lost in no uncertain terms."

In the morning, after eggs and bacon cooked over the campfire, the first major challenge began. The last of the season's calves, born a couple of months before, needed branding and vaccinating. It was to be a humane procedure, Jasper announced.

"Here on the High Lonesome, dehorning is done shortly after birth, as is the castration of male calves." Jasper granted them all a wide, cheerful smile that was distinctly at odds with his gruesome subject. "You won't be dealing with either procedure in this challenge." Made total sense to Brenna. Dehorning was painful for the animal and best done right after birth. As for neutering, no matter how humanely that job was done, it wouldn't make for pretty TV, and the calf wouldn't enjoy it, either.

Jasper kept talking. "And instead of the hot-iron method, we'll be freeze branding, which causes only a momentary sensation of extreme cold and no physical harm or scarring. The hair is frozen off and grows back a lighter color, so the brand is clearly visible from across an open pasture." Once he explained all that, he added, "Before you get started, you'll need to choose your boss."

They voted on that. Fred Franklin, the twins' dad, won the vote. In his late forties, with a steady, confident manner, Fred had a ranch near Buffalo, Wyoming. He knew how to run a branding crew.

Most modern ranchers used four-wheelers to gather the calves and a chute to run them through, with a calf table at the end to hold them in place for the brand.

Not on *The Great Roundup*. They went at it old-school, on horseback.

The gathering and separating of calves from their mamas took forever.

There were reasons. Most of the contestants had experience herding cattle on horseback, but usually it was a job you did on a horse you knew. For the show, they had to use the horses they were given. Brenna got lucky with a great little sorrel mare named Ladygirl. Ladygirl was quick and agile. She would have made a fine barrel horse. Not only did she have the right conformation for a barrel racer, Ladygirl was eager to please and smart, too. That mare had the will to win.

But some of the other High Lonesome horses were understandably skeptical of the strangers riding them. They balked and got fractious. And more than one of the contestants took advantage of the situation, stealing any opportunity to spook another rider's mount.

With filming going on the whole time, cameramen got in the way. Locke kept hollering, "Cut!" so that he could move his minions into position to get a better angle on this or that shot.

Plus, whenever one cowboy got into it with another over some imagined slight or other, Roger would pull the combatants aside for OTFs, where he badgered them about what had happened and how it made them feel.

On the brighter side, Fred made a great boss. He had no problem with letting women do "men's" work. He made sure everyone had a chance to get in on the job, starting with setting up portable panels to form a corral, gathering the two hundred cow-calf pairs in that pasture and driving them into the corral on horseback.

Next, they hooked ropes to the corral panels and used the horses to drag the panels tighter, overlapping them to make an alley leading out.

The cows were more than happy to head for the opening and get free. Brenna and Joey Franklin stationed themselves on foot in the alley, letting the cows go through but turning back the calves. Travis and Steve, both skilled ropers, took positions at the exit and caught any calves that got by her and Joey.

When they stopped for lunch at midday, they had stew and hot bread served up by the hospitality crew.

A few of the men complained at the complete absence of beer. "What's a good branding without the beer?" Dean Fogarth groused.

Trav didn't let him get away with that. "You have enough trouble staying on your horse as it is, Fogarth. The last thing you need is a belly full of beer."

Dean scowled and muttered that the damn horse was a goosey little bugger—and right then the big triangle chuck wagon bell that hung on one of the posts holding up the canteen started clanging.

The bell signaled their first mini challenge. They all had a choice: finish their stew or answer the challenge and get a chance to win some nice little reward.

Brenna considered the possible prizes. A dinner at the lodge, maybe, or a night in a real bed…

She went running with the rest of them—and regretted her decision as soon as she learned that the challenge was to sew buttons on a shirt.

Brenna sucked at sewing. Her mom had taught her

FREE Merchandise is 'in the Cards' for you!

Dear Reader,

We're giving away FREE MERCHANDISE!

Seriously, we'd like to reward you for reading this novel by giving you **FREE MERCHANDISE** worth over $20 retail. And no purchase is necessary!

You see the Jack of Hearts sticker above? Paste that sticker in the box on the Free Merchandise Voucher inside. Return the Voucher today… and we'll send you Free Merchandise!

Thanks again for reading one of our novels—and enjoy your Free Merchandise with our compliments!

Pam Powers

Pam Powers

P.S. Look inside to see what Free Merchandise is **"in the cards"** for you!

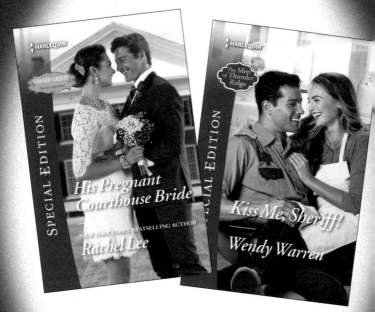

FREE MERCHANDISE VOUCHER

2 FREE BOOKS and **2 FREE GIFTS**

Please send my Free Merchandise, consisting of
2 Free Books and **2 Free Mystery Gifts**.
I understand that I am under no obligation to buy
anything, as explained on the back of this card.

235/335 HDL GLTG

Please Print

FIRST NAME

LAST NAME

ADDRESS

APT.#   CITY

STATE/PROV.   ZIP/POSTAL CODE

Offer limited to one per household and not applicable to series that subscriber is currently receiving.
Your Privacy—The Reader Service is committed to protecting your privacy. Our Privacy Policy is available online at www.ReaderService.com or upon request from the Reader Service. We make a portion of our mailing list available to reputable third parties that offer products we believe may interest you. If you prefer that we not exchange your name with third parties, or if you wish to clarify or modify your communication preferences, please visit us at www.ReaderService.com/consumerschoice or write to us at Reader Service Preference Service, P.O. Box 9062, Buffalo, NY 14240-9062. Include your complete name and address.

NO PURCHASE NECESSARY!

SE-517-FMIVY17

the basics, but she'd never had much interest in getting better at it.

The wranglers passed out the shirts, the buttons and the needles and thread. Each shirt had three buttons missing. You had to replace them and you got points for speed and skill.

Brenna got all three buttons on, eventually. But the finished product was far from stellar. They were four-hole buttons and the thread that showed through was lumpy and uneven. Her tie-off should have been smooth and flat, but it was a hard ball of tangled thread. And Trav's buttons didn't look much better than hers.

Roberta and Steve were a whole other story. They both finished fast. You couldn't tell the buttons they'd sewn on from the ones that had been on the shirts when they started. Brenna felt glad that one of them would surely win.

But no. Summer won. She had the fastest time and the best-looking finished product, at least according to the judges. She laughed and fluttered her eyelashes when Rusty Boles, the judge with the biggest hat, named her the winner. For a prize, she got two hours in a luxury room at the lodge. She could take a long bath and soak the cares of the day away—or watch TV, order up something to eat from hospitality services and have a nap on a real bed.

"Sometimes life is so unfair," Brenna muttered out of the side of her mouth.

Trav put his arm around her and nuzzled her dusty hair. She leaned into him, enjoying his attention way too much. But, hey, never-ending PDAs were a big part of their game. He nibbled her ear. "Disappointed?"

"How did you guess?"

"You're wearing your sulky face."

She stuck out her lower lip and sulked even harder. "I want a bath. And Roberta should have won."

"The judges disagree."

"The judges are such fools. And look at her." She glared at Summer, who was whispering something in Rusty Boles's ear. "Her eyes might pop out of her head if she bats her eyelashes any harder."

Trav nuzzled her hair again. "Meow…"

She playfully shoved him away. "I am never catty." At his low chuckle, she shook a finger at him. "And you'd better watch yourself."

"Or…?"

"You never know the things that I might do."

"Wow, Bren. I'm quaking in my boots."

She leaned in close and pressed a kiss to his bearded jaw, her spirits lifting just from trading a few fond insults with him. "Remember," she warned. "We share a tent, and you have to sleep sometime."

They got half the calves branded and vaccinated that day. Trav and Steve stuck with roping, riding into the knots of milling, bawling calves, setting their ropes for a calf to step into place, then pulling the rope tight on the hind legs and dragging the animal toward the wrestlers, who flipped it and held it in position to get vaccinated, have its ear tag checked and take the brand.

Brenna tried branding and found she had a talent for it. The brands stood in coolers of dry ice. When they stopped bubbling, they were ready to go. Freeze branding was a little trickier than hot branding. She had to hold the frozen iron steadily in place for a good thirty seconds to make sure she killed all the hair pigment cells. She had four other wrestlers on her team to hold the calves steady, and she quickly got the rhythm of the task. Roberta, who'd gone to veterinary school before her cheating dirt-ball ex showed up to mess with her heart, did the vaccinating.

The afternoon stretched into early evening, but they kept after it. Finally, at a little past seven, as the shadows from the mountains crept across the land, Anthony called an end to shooting for that day.

They all turned in their body mics and staggered back to their circle of tents for dinner from a can. Once she'd filled her belly and done her part cleaning up the dishes down at the creek, Brenna grabbed her pack from the tent and headed for the two outdoor showers Real Deal had provided at one of the barns.

Summer, Trav and a few others had been called to the green screen by the canteen for OTFs. Almost everyone else was at the showers, waiting in two lines for a turn in one of the corrugated metal stalls. They discussed the day just passed and the first elimination that would be coming up tomorrow after the remaining calves were branded.

Inside the stall at last, Brenna found there was just one faucet—cold. And she didn't even care. It felt like heaven to wash off the grime. She lathered her hair and rinsed as fast as she could, shivering the whole time. Once she'd dried off, she put on clean clothes and her dusty boots, gathered her things and let the next person have a turn.

Halfway back to the campsite she heard an odd choking sound. Pausing in midstep, she listened—and there it was again, coming from somewhere off to her right, away from the circle of firelight.

And then she heard the sound a third time. A sob, definitely. Someone was crying.

Brenna changed direction, moving as quietly as she could across the rolling, shadowed ground, following the painful, stifled sounds.

Behind a rocky outcropping away from all the other buildings, she found Leah Stone, who was half of the only married couple in the show, crouched behind a boulder. Leah sobbed softly, her head in her hands.

Brenna hesitated. Leah wouldn't have come out here alone in the dark if she wanted company. She and her husband, Seth, mostly kept to themselves. Brenna had hardly shared two words with the woman.

Probably better to just go. As silently as possible, she backed up a step.

But then Leah let out the saddest little moan. It kind of broke Brenna's heart, that lonely, unhappy sound. Really, she couldn't just sneak away without at least making sure Leah was all right.

She took a step forward and then another. By then, she was only a few feet from the crying woman.

Leah must have heard something. Her head shot up. "Who's there?"

Sheepishly, Brenna wiggled her fingers in a wave. "Leah. Hey."

"Oh, God. Brenna…"

"I'm sorry. I should go—"

"No. I… Um. I just…" Leah slowly shook her head. And then, with another sob, she planted her face in her hands again.

Brenna set everything but her towel on one of the boulders and dropped down beside the other woman. "Hey. Hey, now…" She wrapped an arm around Leah.

Leah sobbed harder and huddled closer. Brenna wrapped her in a full hug. "Hey, hey." She stroked Leah's back and smoothed her hair. "It's okay. It'll be okay."

"Oh, no. I don't think it will. I really, really don't."

Brenna wanted to argue, to promise that it would all work out. But she didn't even know what *it* was. So she settled for making soft, reassuring sounds and holding Leah good and close.

Finally, Leah spoke again. "I just wanted a little time, you know, to myself."

"I get that." Brenna tipped up Leah's chin. "You want me to go?"

Leah sniffed. "No, stay. Actually, it feels kind of good to have someone to lean on."

"Here." Brenna used her towel to gently wipe Leah's tear-streaked face. "Sorry, the towel's kind of damp."

"It's cool, though. Feels good." With a ragged little sigh, Leah rested her head on Brenna's shoulder. Brenna reached back and put the towel on the rock behind them. She thought of Fallon, of how she could always get her sister to say what was really bothering her. "Spill."

"Hmm?"

"That's what I say to my sister when I know she wants to tell me what's on her mind but she's trying to be all brave and self-sufficient and not put her troubles on me."

"I *don't* want to put my troubles on you, Brenna. I hardly know you."

"I get that. But sometimes a girl just needs to talk, right?"

"True, but—"

"Come on. Say it."

"Well, can I trust you? I mean, we are in competition."

"Yes, we are." Brenna started to promise that she would keep Leah's confidence. But that wasn't strictly true. She admitted, "Whatever you say, I'll most likely share it with Travis, because I tell him everything." At least, when it came to the show, she did. "But he'll keep it to himself, and I'll never tell anyone else."

"I believe you." With a shaky inhale, Leah lifted her head again. "Too bad Big Brother is always watching." She peered into the darkness, as though she might suddenly spot a hidden camera hanging from a tree.

Brenna shrugged. "I doubt they're recording us here. But you're right. You never know."

Leah put her head back on Brenna's shoulder again and whispered, "I don't think my husband loves me."

"Oh, Leah." Brenna gave the woman a good, tight squeeze.

"I don't think he ever did."

"No…"

"Um-hmm." Leah lifted her head and stared up at the star-scattered sky. "His family's farm was right next to ours. His parents and mine were best friends. I fell in love with him when I was eight. And I never stopped. Who *does* that?"

Brenna smiled to herself, thinking of her six-year-old self declaring undying love to Trav. "Sometimes you just know when it's right." She felt the smile melt right off her face. "Even if *he* doesn't."

Leah gave a sad little nod. "I was always the one pushing him to be with me. We were together straight through high school and when he enrolled at Iowa State, so did I. Everybody expected us to get married, and that worked for me. So we did. And now, after ten years of marriage, he's… Oh, Brenna. He never *talks* to me. He's distant, like a stranger. I thought that getting on this show, having this adventure together, might rekindle the flame, you know? But now I'm afraid there was no flame to start with, at least not for him."

Brenna tried to think of something helpful to say. "Have you talked to him about it?"

"I've tried. I get nowhere. He says everything's fine." She sat up a little straighter. "And I can't believe I'm telling you all this. I don't even *know* you."

Brenna met Leah's eyes and said gently, "I do understand how you feel."

"Because of Travis? You...you think Travis doesn't love you?"

I know he doesn't love me. But she couldn't tell Leah that. Her loyalty to Trav and to the win had to come first. "I'm just saying I get it, that you have your doubts. I, um, have them, too." It was the truth, though not in the way that Leah would assume. Sometimes, especially in the past few days, Brenna wondered if she was getting too attached to her fake fiancé. Sometimes she dreaded the end of the show. Because however it ended, even if they won a million bucks and she could buy the beauty shop from Bee, it wouldn't be easy. They would have to pretend to be engaged for months. And what if Real Deal decided to activate the marriage clause?

Uh-uh. Seriously. She really shouldn't even let herself go there.

Leah asked, "So what do you do when you start doubting?"

"Honestly?"

"Please."

"Denial. Total denial."

Leah actually laughed. "Oh, come on. You're not serious."

"Oh, yes, I am. I tell myself not to think about it. I focus on the moment, on staying in the game. I...keep close with Trav, keep the lines of communication open and remind myself that we're in this together." That didn't sound so bad, did it? And really, it was all true. As far as it went.

"I remember at the final audition at that cowboy bar, the Ace in the Hole?"

"Oh, God." At least the darkness hid her blush of embarrassment. "I really put on a show that night, didn't I?"

"You were great."

"Right."

"I mean it, you *were*—and I remember you said you fell in love with Travis when you were six years old."

Brenna face-palmed. "I have such a big mouth."

"No, really. It was charming and heartfelt, everything you said."

"I went a little crazy that night." *With the help of Homer's magic moonshine.*

"I think you just said what was in your heart. There's nothing wrong with that."

"Leah?" A man's voice—Seth, no doubt—came from the other side of the rocks behind them. "Leah, you out here?"

"Shh." Leah signaled Brenna for silence. And then she leaned close and whispered, "Thank you." Her soft lips brushed Brenna's cheek. "You've made me feel so much better."

"But I only—"

"Leah?" Seth called again.

Leah called back, "Coming!" She leaned into Brenna again and pitched her voice extra low. "Don't you ever doubt Travis. A person only has to watch him watching you to know you're everything to him. That man loves you like nobody's business."

All of a sudden, *she* wanted to cry.

And then Leah swept to her feet. "I'm here, Seth!" She slid around the outcropping and vanished from sight.

"You kissed Summer yesterday, Travis," said Roger. "Why?"

Travis sat in front of the green screen bombarded by golden light, knowing the cameras were picking up every move he made, every slight change in his expression. Two days into filming and already he hated the damn OTFs. And come on, hadn't they already covered this ground yesterday? "Summer kissed *me* yesterday. You'd have to ask her why she did that. I'm in love with my fiancée, and I told Summer so."

"It looked to us like you *almost* kissed Summer back."

"I'm only interested in one woman. That's Brenna O'Reilly. Summer should know that."

"Summer's had her eye on you from the first."

"If Summer's had her eye on me, I didn't notice."

"She's a beauty. And so seductive. It's crystal clear she'd like to make time with you."

"I have a feeling Summer would like to make time with a lot of guys. She should pick one of them and leave me the hell alone."

"Why are you so riled up, Travis? Does Summer

pose more of a temptation for you than you're willing to admit?"

Travis had the urge to leap from his camp chair and go after Roger, bust him a good one right in the chops. But that would only be giving the producer exactly what he was after.

Which, come to think of it, was exactly what Travis was supposed to do. Play the game, get emotional. Start a fight.

But what was it Bren said last night? That Summer should play a *better* game?

Maybe *he* ought to take his fake fiancée's advice. Travis drew a slow breath and ordered his heart rate to even out. "I'll tell you what temptation is. My girl. *She's* a pure temptation. I waited a long time, years, to finally have my chance with Bren. At first, she was too young for me. And for way too long, as the good Lord and all of Rust Creek Falls knows, I was dead set on never settling down. I don't deserve her. I never did. But somehow she loves me, anyway. And so we're together now. No other woman can even compare. And yeah, I say that from experience. I've been with other girls. I've had my wild times. Now there's only one woman I want to get crazy with. That's why that woman has my ring on her finger. That's why I can't wait to make Brenna my wife."

When Travis got back to the tent, Brenna sat on her bedroll in her Bushwacker T-shirt, braiding that gorgeous red hair of hers by lantern light.

She gave him a soft smile as he ducked between the tent flaps. "How was the OTF?" She wore no bra. The T-shirt was several sizes too big for her, but it couldn't disguise the natural movement of her breasts beneath the worn fabric as she worked on her braid.

God, she smelled good, all clean and fresh. He bent close to get a whiff of her hair. Apples and honey. He wanted to touch it, to stroke his hand down and grab the end of that braid. He would give it a tug. She would laugh and slap at him, order him to stop. So he would capture her obstinate chin and tip her lips up to claim a long, sweet kiss.

Because that's who they were now. At least for the next six weeks or so. Brenna and Travis, deeply in love and planning on forever side by side.

"Trav?"

"Um?"

"The OTF?"

He grabbed his pack. "I've decided I hate OTFs."

She chuckled as she wrapped an elastic around the end of the finished braid. "Wait. Let me guess. They came after you about Summer again?"

"No surprise, huh?"

"Not even a little."

"The good news is I think I shut them up, at least for now. I told them all about you. How you're the only woman in the world for me."

She flipped her braid back over her shoulder. "My hero," she whispered in twangy drawl. "You're such a total romantic." She pretended to shiver with pleasure.

He shoved his pack against the side of the tent, took her by her strong, slim shoulders and pushed her onto her back, hiking a knee over her so he had her pinned between his thighs.

She blinked up at him looming above her on his

hands and knees and whispered, "Okay. What's the game?"

He bent his head and kissed her—a quick one, to start. Her mouth tasted like peppermint. She must have already brushed her teeth. "I need a shower."

She arched an eyebrow at him. "Not the answer to my question."

He tipped his head toward the lantern. "You've got the lantern on. Anyone outside can see our shadows in here..."

She got it then. Her mouth formed a soft O and her eyes shone the brightest, clearest blue.

He bent close again. "I think I need to kiss you— even if I do smell like the back end of a rode-hard horse."

She licked her pink lips. Damn. He couldn't wait to kiss them again. "It's very manly, how you smell."

"Manly. I'll take it."

With a happy little sigh, she lifted her soft arms and wrapped them around his neck. They felt so good there. He could almost wish she would never let go. "And of course you should kiss me," she whispered. "Because I've got the lantern on and anyone could be looking. And if they *are* looking, they need to see how we can't keep our hands off each other."

"It's a difficult job, all this kissing," he replied, straight-faced and solemn. "But it's *our* job, and we *have* to do it."

"Less talk." She made a growling sound. "More action."

He smiled at her and she returned it, right before he lowered his head and his mouth touched hers.

A soft, eager moan escaped her. And she opened so sweetly, letting him in.

Heaven and peppermint. She tasted so good. He wanted to lower his body to hers, press her down into the bedroll, reach for the hem of that faded T-shirt and slowly ease it upward, uncovering her slowly, inch by smooth inch...

Her fingers stroked his nape, and another moan escaped her. She breathed his name into his mouth. "Trav..."

His body burned. He ached, he was so hard and ready for her.

This was getting dangerous.

This was getting far too real.

"Come down here." She wrapped her hand around his nape and tugged a little. "You're too far away."

He was. Way too far. No doubt about it. He slid an arm under her and turned her as he lowered his body. Straightening his legs, he rolled them both to their sides.

"Better." She stroked the hair at his temples, rubbed his rough cheek. "I like your beard, the way you keep it short and scruffy. It's sexy. And it feels so good, a little scratchy and yet silky, too."

"That does it. I'll never shave again."

"Works for me."

He should stop. But he didn't want to stop. He kissed her some more as he trailed his hand up over the curve of her hip and down into the tender valley of her waist.

His hand was still on top of her shirt. He promised himself he would keep it there.

But then he cheated. Just a little. He ran his palm back over her hip again, going lower that time, down along the cool flesh of her bare thigh. Her skin felt so good, so smooth and perfect. *Mine*. The word filled his head. *Made just for me.* He curved his rough fingers around the tender cove behind her knee and tugged.

She giggled. He drank in the sweet sound as she took his cue, lifting her leg, wrapping it over his thigh. Her heel brushed his calf, burning like a brand even through the heavy denim of his jeans. He yearned to press himself hard and tight against her. To get rid of that T-shirt, strip off his dusty clothes and bury himself in the sweet heat of her body.

Somehow, he made himself break the mind-blowing, never-ending kiss. They stared at each other. He let his gaze wander, over her flushed cheeks and her swollen mouth and those eyes that glittered so bright, teasing him, inviting him.

"Do we have to stop?" she whispered. He made himself nod. "Why? Let's turn off the lamp, Trav. Let's see where this takes us."

He balled his hands into fists to keep from grabbing her again. "You're making me crazy."

She reached for the lamp. The tent went dark. "Are you sure that's a bad thing?"

Chapter Eight

"Right now, I'm not sure of anything." Travis uttered the words like a confession into the darkness between them.

But they were a lie. He was sure of one thing: he wanted her.

And that wanting was growing. Every hour he was near her, he wanted her more.

She was a handful, Brenna O'Reilly. Any man would have a hell of a time trying to tame her.

But then again, he didn't want to tame her. He wanted her *untamed*. Wanted her just as she was and always had been— a little bit wild, sometimes kind of crazy. Beautiful. Strong. Willful and true.

She moved in the darkness. The sweet scent of her drifted closer. And then she framed his face between her two cool hands. "Think about it." Her breath touched his lips. "Think *real* hard."

"Bren." It came out on a groan.

And then she moved again—away from him, damn it.

He didn't realize she'd grabbed his pack until she shoved it into his arms. "Oof."

"Go on, cowboy. Have that shower."

"Bren…"

And she bent close and kissed him again, a sweet brush of her mouth on his. "Go." She gave a low laugh. "Before I grab you and have my evil way with you."

When he got back to the tent, the light was still off. He could make out the shape of her in her sleeping bag. He stripped down and slid into his own bag.

"'Night, Trav." Her voice was thick and lazy, hovering on the edge of sleep.

"'Night." His cold shower had taken the edge off his need for her. Now he just felt good to be lying there beside her in the dark.

He laced his hands behind his head and stared up into the darkness and thought about condoms. He had one, because even a guy who'd sworn off women should have the sense to carry a condom just in case. It was in his battered wallet in the bottom of his pack. One condom in a creased-up wrapper. It was probably out of date by now.

And that was probably a good thing. The next time kissing her threatened to get out of hand, he would just remind himself that you couldn't trust an old condom with a creased-up wrapper and he needed to behave himself.

Yeah. Right. Sure. That would work.

"Trav? You still awake?" Her sweet, sleepy voice tempted him out of the dark.

He gave her a low "Um" for an answer.

"I've been thinking…"

"Um?"

Her whisper went lower. "You may be right. About the sex? We probably shouldn't go there. We need to, you know, keep our heads on straight, focus on the game. Right?"

"You're right." They were just about the hardest two words he'd ever said.

"You're…okay with that?"

"I'm good," he lied. "Go back to sleep."

They finished branding the calves before noon the next day and filmed the first elimination in front of the canteen right after lunch.

Brenna stood next to Trav, who'd seemed kind of distant all day. Was he upset with her? Did he think she was a big tease or something, to be all over him one minute and then change her mind?

Did they need to talk it over?

Ugh. It had been hard enough telling him she'd had second thoughts. And now, to bring it up again?

Not her idea of a fun conversation.

But still. They needed to be strong together, as a team. And how could they be strong if there were simmering resentments between them? They had to keep straight, stay on point, be clearheaded and ready to face whatever the game threw at them.

So okay. In the interest of keeping things straight between them, if he still seemed distant tonight, she would bring it up to him and they would talk it out.

And then she spotted Summer maybe eight feet away, on the far side of Seth and Leah. The blonde kept sliding glances at Trav. Planning her next seduction attempt, no doubt. Brenna flashed the other woman a bright smile and leaned into Travis. He glanced down at her, and she tipped up her face for a quick kiss.

He gave it, brushing his lips across hers, lightening her heart, making her smile.

If he had been annoyed with her, he seemed to be getting over it.

When she slid another glance at Summer, the blonde was facing front, pretending to care what Jasper was saying.

Dag Dodson, the judge with the medium-sized hat, announced the three top scores in the branding challenge. "Steve Simon, Travis Dalton and Fred Franklin, step right up, please."

No one was that surprised when Jasper declared Fred the winner. They all applauded as the twins' dad claimed his immunity bracelet from the carved box. Fred had been the perfect boss—fair, considerate and firm, with a good handle on how the job should be done. Brenna would be proud to work for him anytime.

"And now," said Jasper, suddenly solemn as a preacher at a funeral, "it's time to say goodbye to one of you."

The three judges burst into a song. It was an oldie, by Woody Guthrie, "So Long, It's Been Good to Know Yuh."

Those old guys were good, too, in perfect harmony. They sang one verse and the chorus. Trav returned to Brenna's side as Rusty Boles whipped out a harmonica and played it soft and low and lonesome sounding.

The third judge stepped up to read the names of the

three lowest scorers. Brenna grabbed for Trav's hand. He wrapped his warm fingers around hers nice and tight. She really didn't think she'd end up in the bottom three, but she couldn't be sure.

And she was right. The judge didn't call her name.

Not surprisingly, Dean Fogarth was among the three. He got lucky, though. Another guy, a truck driver from Colorado, was the first to go. The judges sang another Woody Guthrie song, and the truck driver was sent to take down his tent, grab his gear and move to the lodge.

As one of the wranglers led him off, another clanged the chuck wagon bell.

Jasper laughed. "That's right, folks. It's your big chance to take a mini challenge. Who's in? Everybody? That's what I like to see."

It was a cooking challenge that time.

Skillet chili and corn bread. Each of them had to have their own recipe in their head or know how to fake it. With a flourish, Jasper gestured them all into the canteen, where their choices of ingredients were arrayed on two long tables, including several big bottles of Jack Daniel's whiskey—for the chili, supposedly.

Trav grabbed one of the bottles and then just stood there, at a loss.

Good thing Maureen O'Reilly made the best corn bread chili in three counties. And she'd taught her daughters well.

Trav looked at Brenna hopefully.

She put him out of his misery. "Yes, I can make my mother's chili."

"Score!" He waved his bottle gleefully.

"But her recipe doesn't call for whiskey."

"I'm not letting go of this bottle. See, I always cook with whiskey. Some of it even ends up in the food."

"Har-har. Just do what I do."

He wrapped an arm around her neck and yanked her close. "Damn, you're gorgeous." He laid a big smacker square on her mouth. "And you can cook. I am a lucky, lucky man."

She laughed and ducked away, feeling good about everything at that moment. He really didn't seem the least distant now. Maybe they didn't need to talk, after all.

Trav stuck close to her as they started on the mini challenge, grabbing the same ingredients she gathered, taking a space next to her at one of the prep tables, watching everything she did and then doing the same.

A couple of hours later, the judges started tasting.

Turned out old Wally Wilson used to cook for more than one outfit. The old man knew his corn bread chili. And he had experience making it over an open fire.

Wally won. His prize was a whole night at the lodge in a real bed.

He tipped his hat to the judges. "These old bones thank you kindly."

Travis's entry turned out burned on the bottom. But Brenna's chili was pretty darn good, if she did say so herself. They ate their entries for dinner. Brenna and Wally had plenty to share with Trav and the other bad cooks.

After the meal, Wally happily followed one of the wranglers off to claim his prize.

Not much of the Jack Daniel's had ended up in chili—which Brenna assumed had been the plan all along. She'd watched enough reality TV to know that when contestants got tipsy, good TV happened.

Everyone hung around the fire as night came on. They were unmic'd by then, but Roger had put a couple of cameramen on them, and there were also cameras mounted in the nearby trees. Nobody seemed to care that they were being filmed. Already, having a camera watching their every move had become normal for all of them, just the way that they lived.

They sipped whiskey from their tin cups as wranglers came to collect them, one by one, for their turns in front of the green screen.

When all the OTFs were done, most of the guys remained by the fire sipping whiskey, telling tall tales of their ranching and rodeo adventures. Roberta and Steve had gone off for a walk together. Brenna headed for the showers. When she got back, Trav showed no inclination to budge from his camp chair.

She thought about whispering to him that she needed to talk to him. But did she really? By afternoon, he'd seemed to be over whatever had been bothering him. No reason to ruin his buzz. They could talk later. Tomorrow night or the next.

Yeah, it might be a bad idea to leave him alone out there with the other men, a couple of the women she didn't know at all—and Summer. But she wasn't his babysitter, and she couldn't really blame him for wanting to get a little loose, shoot the breeze with the other guys.

Brenna ducked into the tent and shut the flaps. In the dark, she wriggled out of her clothes and into her sleep shirt and crawled into her sleeping bag.

Outside, she heard laughter from the men at the fire and thought of her childhood, of summer nights outside around a campfire, the glow of firelight warming the smiling faces of the ones she loved and—

A shout had her sitting straight up in her sleeping bag.

She scuttled to the tent flaps and peeked out.

Dean Fogarth and Randy Teasdale, a horse rancher from Idaho, circled each other on the far side of the fire. Dean threw a blow and connected. Randy landed on his butt in the dirt.

"Get up," growled Dean.

Randy grabbed Dean's boot and gave it a tug. Dean went down, too. The men rolled in the dirt together, grunting and punching each other.

Summer stood not far away, watching with an unreadable expression on her pretty face. The cameras were rolling.

Trav sat on Brenna's side of the fire, maybe twenty feet from their tent. Brenna threw a small rock and hit the back of his camp chair with it.

He twisted to look over his shoulder at her. "Hey, sleepyhead." He gave her a lazy, liquored-up grin.

"What's going on?"

He raised his tin cup to her. "Dean and Randy are havin' a li'l disagreement."

"Over Summer?"

Travis laughed. "How'd you guess? C'mon out, baby. Time to party."

Baby. Why did it sound so good when he called her that? She was definitely tempted to pull on her jeans and join him.

But no. Not tonight. She shook her head and retreated to the relative safety of the tent.

The fight went on for a while. She heard a whole

bunch of scuffling and a lot of angry swearing, words that were never going to make it onto network TV.

After the fight, somebody brought out a guitar. They all sang together—rowdy cowboy songs at first, "Friends in Low Places" and "All My Rowdy Friends Are Coming Over Tonight." Eventually they slowed things down and sang some great old ballads.

Somewhere in the middle of "Down in the Valley," Brenna dropped off to sleep.

"Bren? You 'sleep?" She felt a tap on her shoulder. "Bren?"

"Not anymore," she grumbled, rolling onto her back and blinking up into the darkness at the silhouette of Trav bending over her. "What time is it?"

A burst of whiskey breath hit her face. "Late. S'very, very late."

"Who won the fight?"

"I think they called it a draw. Summer got disgusted and stormed off."

"I don't really get it. What was the fight *about*, exactly?"

"Hmm. Two hotheaded drunk cowboys an' a flirty woman. 'Nuff said."

"Fascinating."

"As in you mean, it's not. Right?"

"Trav?"

"Um?"

"Time to lie down in your sleeping bag and get some sleep." She started to turn over.

"Wait."

"What?"

"Well, I got my boots off and got in my bag and then I jus' couldn't stan' not t' say 'night to you."

"You're drunk," she whispered gently.

"Unfort'nately, s'true."

"Well, good night, then." Again, she tried to roll back onto her side.

That time he held her in place with a hand on her shoulder. "Aw. Don' go..."

She stifled a chuckle. "Oh, Trav. You're going to be so sorry tomorrow."

She watched his white teeth flash in the darkness. "Oh, yes, I am. And you are so beaut'ful, Bren."

Something sweet and warm uncurled in her belly and she teased, "It's pitch-dark in here. You can't even see me."

"I don' need t' see you. I got you in here." He pointed in the general direction of his head. "Jus' how you look, with your skin like cream an' your red hair all sleek or, like lately, with it crazy curly so you gripe about it all the time an' put it in a braid down your back. With that bold smile on your mouth and those gold freckles so cute on the bridge of your nose. And those eyes, Bren. Where'd you get those eyes that are blue as the ocean sometimes and sometimes like a stormy sky?"

"Oh, Trav. What you just said? *That's* beautiful."

"What I'm tryin' to tell you is that I see you even when I don't see you. Does that make any sense? Nope," he answered his own question. "No sense at all. But it's the truth, anyway. You are burned in my brain. Like a brand, y'know?"

Like a brand. Her heart went to mush. She tried re-ally hard to remember that he was drunk and he probably wouldn't recall any of this tomorrow. "You need to get some—"

"No. Lissen."

"Trav—"

"I shouldna got drunk, I know it. Ver' unprofessional of me. But I needed to blow off a li'l steam, you know?"

"It's fine. I get it. Now, just go to—"

"Bren. There's been no one for me. Not for over a year."

"Trav, you don't have to—"

"Jus' wait. Let me finish, 'kay?"

She was torn—curious about what he might reveal, and also oddly protective of him, of his privacy. In the morning, he might very well regret that the whiskey had loosened his tongue tonight.

"Yer quiet," he whispered. "So I'm gonna take that as a yes. Bren, you know how I've always been kind of busy with the ladies."

Busy with the ladies? She couldn't help it. She laughed.

"You laugh," he said with great solemnity. "But it's really not funny. I'm sick an' tired of bein' the hot player of Rus' Creek Falls. An' tha's why I haven' been with anyone in a year—not since this good-looking woman from Denver came lookin' for me."

The last thing she wanted was to hear about him and some other woman. "Trav, I—"

"Shh. There's a point to this. Jus' give me a chance to get there, will ya please?" He waited for her low hum of reluctant agreement before he went on. "This woman, she asked around town about me. Somebody gave her my number. We met up the next night, early, at the Ace. I asked her to dinner. And she said, 'Oh, honey. I don't need dinner. Le's jus' get a room.' I took her to a nice hotel I know in Kalispell. And afterward, when she was getting dressed to leave, she tol' me I was exac'ly as advertised, as good as her girlfriend said I would be."

"Oh, no." Brenna reached up in the darkness and put her hand against his beard-rough cheek. "I'm so sorry, Trav. What a horrible thing to say to you."

"Well, ackshually, she did mean it as a compliment. When I was younger, what she said wouldn'ta bothered me at all. I was jus' out for a good time back then, an' I didn' care what anybody thought. But lately, well, it had started to get so it wasn' much of a thrill, spendin' a night with a stranger. The past few years, I'd been wantin' more but not exac'ly sure how to go about gettin' it. A man acts like a player fer long enough, that's all any woman sees when she looks his way. An' that's why what that woman said that night was kind of a wake-up call. Y'know what I mean?"

She stroked the hair at his temple. "Tell me her name. I'll find her and beat the crap out of her for you."

He gave a low laugh. "You al'ays were a bloodthirsty li'l thing—an' I mean it. S'okay, really."

"You know you'll always be a hero to me."

He let out another big gust of whiskey-scented breath. "Thanks, Bren."

"It's the truth." And it was. It really was.

"An' y'know, a wake-up call ain't necessarily a bad thing. 'Cause I think it was time."

"Time?"

"Yeah, time to knock off chasin' women. And it hasn't been that tough, you know? I guess I've already had all the meaningless sex I'll ever need."

She almost laughed, but it really wasn't funny. He might be drunk, but she knew he was telling her something he wouldn't tell just anyone. He trusted her, and she treasured that trust. She cleared her throat. "Well, then. Good to know."

"An' I only said all that to tell you…" The sentence wandered off, unfinished.

"To tell me what?"

"Well, Bren, you said we *should* and then you said we *shouldn't*. An' I want you so bad I jus' want to give in, figure out some excuse to hold you and kiss you and not to stop there. I want to be with you when it's jus' you and me, alone, with nobody lookin'. Because it wouldn' be meaningless with you, Bren. With you, I know, it would be real."

Tears burned her eyes at such beautiful words.

But he wasn't finished. "Too bad there is no excuse, an' I need to remember that. We got a plan, and gettin' naked together ain't part of it. An' that's why I, well, I jus' wanna say, you were right the second time. We *shouldn't*."

His rough, warm hand touched her face, the lightest breath of a caress and then gone. She wanted to lift up, follow that touch, wanted him to *keep* touching her, wanted him to never, ever stop.

"It would be wrong," he whispered, "to go gettin' *really* intimate, you an' me. Reality TV is as *un*real as it gets and you 'n' me need to keep our heads about us. I know that. I get that. But that doesn' mean I'm not crazy for you, Bren."

"I'm…"

"Yeah?"

…*crazy for you, too*. She longed to say it. Because she was. Really, truly long-gone crazy.

Seriously, who did she think she was kidding for all

these years? She'd fallen for him when she was six years old. And all her later declarations to the contrary, she'd never stopped yearning to have him for her own. She could lie to herself all she wanted.

But lies wouldn't change the truth of the matter. She'd tried being with other guys. First with Davey Hart, her steady guy in high school. Davey had been her first, and she'd sworn she would love him forever. They broke up when he went off to college in Texas. It just hadn't been that hard to see him go.

And then there was Alan Schultz. She and Alan had even lived together in Missoula, while she went to cosmetology school. But when he ended it, she'd had to face the fact that she'd never really loved him.

Since then, there'd been no one. Why bother? Without the right person to do it with, she didn't care all that much about sex.

"Bren?"

"What?"

"You didn' finish. You said, 'I'm...' an' then you stopped."

"Go to sleep, Trav."

"Bren..."

"Go to sleep."

He loomed above her for a second more. Then, with a cheerful, "Okay," he flopped back to his own bedroll. He let out a groan and asked woozily, "How come the tent is spinnin'?"

"Close your eyes."

"Ugh. No. Bad idea."

Was he going to be sick? Dear Lord, she hoped not.

But then he whispered, "'Night, Bren." And he instantly started snoring.

She hiked up on an elbow and bent over him. "Trav?"

He just went on snoring, dead to the world.

So she dropped back to her side of the tent, closed her eyes and tried not to think about what had just happened.

Like a brand.

All these years she'd gotten along fine, she and her well-accustomed, comfortable denial. She'd told herself she was over him—that really, there was nothing to *get* over. It was a childhood crush, no big deal. He was an honorary big brother to her, a family friend with a strong protective streak when it came to her.

They understood each other, she and Travis. And what they understood was that nothing was ever going to happen between them. He couldn't be tamed. And neither could she.

They probably should have thought twice before faking an engagement to get on *The Great Roundup.* They probably should have considered that if there *was* any spark between them, pretending to be lovers who couldn't keep their hands off each other was no way to avoid starting a fire.

Now they were into it and into it deep. With a little help from his good friend Jack Daniel's, he'd admitted far too much tonight —and she had loved every slurred word of his beautiful, ridiculous declaration.

She'd loved it because she loved *him.*

"I love him." She mouthed the words into the darkness, careful not to give them sound, though the man snoring at her side probably wouldn't notice if she shouted them at the top of her lungs.

I love Travis Dalton. It was real and it was true, and there was no use continuing to deny it.

Did she think she could tame him?

Highly unlikely.

Was she going to get her poor heart broken?

Oh, it was very possible.

But did she want to take this fake love affair all the way to the end anyway, no matter how it all turned out?

Oh, yes, she did. If she ever hoped to have a chance with him, this was it, now, here at High Lonesome Guest Ranch on *The Great Roundup*.

And they didn't call her the bold, chance-taking, troublemaking O'Reilly for nothing.

She loved Travis Dalton.

She *wanted* Travis Dalton.

And one way or another, for however long it lasted, she was bound to have him.

Chapter Nine

Brenna planned to make her move the next day--and no, she didn't know exactly what that move would be. But she expected at least to have a real talk with him when they were alone in their tent at the end of the day.

Travis looked green when they got up at dawn. He'd done it to himself by answering what all the guys were jokingly calling "the whiskey challenge." Still, she felt sorry for him.

The Great Roundup didn't call a day off just because most of the men were hungover. They began the next major challenge right after breakfast.

The task? To cut and bale hay in a series of far pastures. Actually, haying involved more than just cutting and baling. There was also tedding—spreading the hay out in the field to dry. And windrowing--raking the spread hay into rows to ready it for baling

They got to use machinery for this three-day process, taking turns on the tractors provided. All that first day Brenna worried that Travis might just keel over—or worse, roll a tractor and end up injured or dead. But somehow, he made it through and even managed to hold up his end.

And when they crawled into their bags that night, he was sound asleep before she could even think of how to begin to tell him that she'd changed her mind *again* about the two of them becoming lovers.

The haying challenge continued for two more days after that. An elimination followed. Dean Fogarth, who had somehow managed never once to get behind the wheel of a tractor during any part of the hay-making process, said goodbye that time. Travis won that challenge and claimed his immunity bracelet.

And that night, when Brenna got him alone, he was his old self again. They joked together and talked a little of what the next challenge might be.

But when she tried to bring up the two of them and how she'd like to take this fake relationship to a whole new level, he looked straight in her eyes and said, "I think we settled that, didn't we, Bren? I think we decided we shouldn't go there."

And what could she say to that?

She let it go that night.

And the next, and the next after that.

The challenges continued, one after another. They worked long days, driving cattle to higher pastures in the pouring rain. They slept out in the open two nights on the way up there, taking turns watching the herd, huddled under tarps against the downpour.

The sun came out when they reached their destination. Everyone cheered, including the crew, who'd struggled constantly to keep the cameras and sound equipment dry. Jasper announced the next challenge— to choose a partner and build a makeshift shelter out of what they could scavenge on the land.

Brenna and Travis got right to work. She sent him looking for a long, sturdy pole branch and prop sticks while she scouted locations. At the edge of the wide, rolling meadow, a trail wound up into the trees. She followed that trail until she came out on a rocky promontory jutting over a flat space. There, in the shelter of the cliff, she and Trav built a leaf hut lean-to, which she'd learned to make back in her 4-H days. The spot had good drainage, so they stayed reasonably dry that night.

The wind came up and the temperature dropped, so they stripped to their driest layer of T-shirts and underwear, zipped their bags together and slept all wrapped around each other. Brenna grinned to herself as she cuddled in close to him. She smelled like a lathered horse and her hair had bits of dirt and leaves in it. That night, having sex with him was the last thing on her mind. She felt only gratitude for the warmth of him all around her, for the strength in the arms that held her so close.

Brenna took the win on the shelter challenge—for choosing the best spot and knowing how to build the hut. After she'd put on her immunity bracelet, yet another contestant, a woman that time, went back to the lodge for good.

Jasper assigned two mini challenges that day. And the next morning, they headed down the mountain to their little tent village, which kept getting smaller after each elimination.

The days seemed to bleed together, one into the other.

They mended fences, burned weeds in ditches, went hunting for stray livestock and answered the endless mini challenges, from starting fires without matches to chopping wood, target shooting and doing laundry in the creek. Everyone complained that the mini challenge prizes had gotten chintzier. They were a camp pillow or an extra fry pan for cooking. By then, everyone longed for a night at the lodge. Too bad that lately the only way to get that was to get eliminated.

Brenna worked up her nerve and tried again to talk to Trav about the two of them. She got nowhere. Trav reminded her gently to focus on the win.

She decided that maybe he was right. Maybe, if she was going to make a play for him, she just ought to wait till filming was over and they were back home. Back home, at least he wouldn't be able to tell her she needed to keep her focus on the game.

By the last week of June, half the contestants had been sent to the lodge to stay. Bren and Trav, Roberta and Steve, Seth and Leah, Fred and the twins, Wally and Summer Knight remained in the game. Travis said they were all living proof that alliances made the difference. Everyone still in the running had someone they could count on.

"Except Wally and Summer," Brenna reminded him.

"Yeah, well, Wally gets along with everyone and Summer's good at the game."

Oh, yes, she was. Summer had the skill set to avoid elimination in a challenge. And she caused plenty of conflict, which didn't make her any friends but sure made for interesting TV.

The next day Seth Stone tumbled down a ravine and broke his leg, a messy compound fracture. They sent a helicopter for him from the hospital in Kalispell. The med techs took a stretcher down into the narrow canyon. They stabilized the injured leg and strapped him in for the ride up the steep bank to level ground. Travis, Fred, Joey and Rob helped to carry him up out of the ravine.

As they got ready to load him into the helicopter, Leah hovered close to him, clutching his hand. "I want to go with you."

He brought her fingers to his lips and kissed them. "Stick with it, sweetheart. Win it for both of us. I know it's what you want."

Leah's tears spilled over. "Seth, what I want is *you*. I love you so."

"I love you, too, honey. Always have, always will."

"You, um…you sure? Because lately, I…"

He searched her face. "What?"

She hesitated, but then he kissed the back of her hand and she busted to it. "Well, I wonder if maybe you're a little bit sorry that you married me, if maybe you have regrets that you were never really…free."

"Aw, sweetheart. Come here."

She bent closer and he asked, "What about you? Are you sad you never got your chance to be free?"

Leah gasped. "Of course not. You've always been the only guy for me."

"And you're the only girl for me. Honey, how could I be sorry? I've loved you since you were eight years old."

"Oh, Seth." She sniffed back tears. "Say it one more time."

"I love you, Leah Stone. There's no one else for me."

"Seth." She bent even closer and pressed her eager lips to his.

The cameras captured all of it. And Leah and Seth

could not have cared less that the cameras were rolling and everyone was watching. They had eyes only for each other.

After the med techs loaded the injured man onto the helicopter and took him away, Leah stood in the middle of the cleared space, looking up, watching the chopper vanish into the clear afternoon sky.

Brenna went to her. "Leah…"

With a cry, Leah grabbed on and hugged Brenna close. "He does love me," she whispered prayerfully. "He truly does."

"No doubt about it."

"I want to be with him. I *need* to be with him. I can't concentrate on winning when my husband needs me. I…I have to leave the show."

Brenna took both her hands. "Go talk to Roger. See what he says." Their body mics and the ever-present cameras had recorded every word. Brenna had a feeling that Roger, Anthony and the rest of them were loving the drama.

And that Real Deal Entertainment would let Leah go.

An hour later, after a final OTF in the middle of the cleared space where the helicopter had landed, a wrangler took Leah to the lodge to gather her and Seth's belongings. Brenna and Travis took down her tent for her. Gerry would drive her to the hospital in Kalispell.

The next morning Jasper gathered the remaining nine of them together for a one-day challenge.

They all got to show off their roping skills with a series of roping tricks, starting with the basics: coiling, building a loop, refining the loop and coils, swinging and catching. First, they roped a dummy. And by the end of the day, they each had to rope and tie a calf. The top ropers in the group—Trav, Steve, Wally and Fred—blew the rest of them away. But no one was a complete greenhorn at the job. Bren thought she was good enough to avoid elimination.

That night at the canteen, Trav won the roping challenge and claimed his immunity bracelet. Joey Franklin packed up and followed a wrangler to the lodge.

Now they were eight.

And the next day, everything changed. They met at the canteen for the morning's challenge and Jasper announced that they would be sent out in teams of two, each team to accomplish a different goal.

"And we want to switch things up a little," Jasper said with a wink. "This time, we'll be choosing your partners for you." He paired Brenna with Steve. Roberta got Fred Franklin. Old Wally and Rob Franklin were together.

And Travis got partnered with Summer.

Brenna told herself she would work hard with Steve and keep her mind off her own pointless jealousy. She wasn't even going to consider what Summer might get up to, given a whole day alone with Trav.

Yeah, Trav had refused to take what he and Brenna shared to the next level. But that didn't mean he would say yes to Summer. Bren and Trav had a strong alliance, she told herself. No way would he let Summer mess with that.

Brenna and Steve's challenge was to clean out one of the barns.

They got to work shoveling manure and clearing out moldy hay. They gathered rusty, abandoned tools into the empty crates someone had conveniently left piled against a back wall.

At noon, they stopped work for sandwiches provided by hospitality services—everyone but Travis and Summer. Wherever they were and whatever they were doing, apparently they couldn't afford to stop and return to the canteen for food.

At one, Steve and Brenna went back to the barn. The chuck wagon bell rang at a little after two. They were in pretty good shape in the barn, with most of the job done, so they both answered the mini challenge.

As did everyone else—except Summer and Travis, who were still off who knew where doing God knew what. The mini challenge was to make a pot of campfire coffee.

Steve came up beside Brenna, and as if he read her mind, he said, "They're probably too far out to ride in for a mini challenge."

Roberta leaned close. "Nothing to worry about, Bren."

Brenna put on a big smile. "Do I look worried?"

Steve and Roberta agreed that she didn't.

The coffee challenge went fast. Wally won, as he tended to do anytime campfire cookery was involved. Jasper said they could all have a ten-minute coffee break. "And what d' you know, folks? The coffee's fresh made." They each had a cup and then went back to work.

At the end of the day, when the rest of them were already gathered at the canteen, Summer and Travis finally rode in. Their clothes were wet and splattered with mud. Summer was laughing, flashing her dimples at Trav.

A two-man camera team and an assistant director

trailed after them. Film of their day's work would have been transmitted back to camp for the judges to view. The highlights would probably end up on the show.

Anthony signaled the newcomers to join the rest of them. Trav and Summer dismounted, and a couple of wranglers took the horses away.

Summer laughed again and wrapped both hands around Travis's arm. "Whoa, what a day, huh?"

Brenna knew her role too well by now. For the sake of the game and her part in the story, she really ought to do something——something lighthearted and cute, if possible. She ought to run to Travis, grab him away from Summer and kiss him senseless, maybe.

Or she could go raw, put on some sort of jealous display to keep the story moving——the story of lovebirds Brenna and Travis and that man-stealer Summer.

But no. It all felt way too real, and that wasn't fun.

Because she *was* jealous, and she hated that—despised it, even. She'd always been kind of a hothead, and she needed to keep a lid on that emotion. If she didn't hold herself in check, she'd put a whupping on the rodeo star. Just what she needed, to end up on national TV catfighting over Trav. Her mom would never forgive her.

Uh-uh. The game had turned too real. And for the moment anyway, Brenna refused to play.

Instead, she faced front and showed the cameras nothing. When Trav appeared at her side, she managed to give him what she hoped passed for a welcoming smile. He draped an arm across her shoulders and pulled her close to press his lips to her hair. She felt his breath across her skin, the wonderful, hard weight of his arm on her shoulder. He smelled of mud and man. Longing burned through her.

Somehow, she kept her expression composed. She laughed on cue when Jasper cracked a corny joke, sang along with the judges when they burst into a Tim Mc-Graw song.

There was no winner that night, and no one got eliminated. Jasper announced that points would accrue in a series of daylong challenges and the next elimination would be called with no warning.

They were excused to rustle up dinner over the campfire, head for the showers and take turns at the green screen. Brenna's OTF was all about Summer and Trav and what she thought the two of them were doing out alone together the whole day long.

She answered in flat, short sentences: "I don't know" and "You should ask them."

"You seem upset, Brenna."

"I'm not upset in the least."

"Do you have anything you'd like to say to Summer?"

"I have nothing at all to say to Summer."

"Anything to say to Travis?"

She aimed a giant smile at the camera. "Travis, I love you more than words can ever say."

"You're pissed at me, aren't you?" Trav whispered.

He'd come back from the showers a few minutes before. They were alone in their dark tent. She couldn't stop thinking of Leah and Seth, of the love and honesty between them at the end.

"Bren?"

She turned her head away from him and closed her eyes. "Get some sleep."

"Come on."

"What."

"Just tell me. Are you pissed at me?"

"Just leave it, will you please?"

"Nothing happened with Summer. You gotta know that." He launched into a way too detailed description of what he and the blonde had done all day, including tracking a heifer who'd lacerated her teat on a barbwire fence. "To make it all more fun, that heifer had run into a patch of blackberry canes. It was a mess." He fell silent.

Apparently, she was supposed to say something. "What do you want from me, Trav?"

"You know I've got no interest in Summer Knight."

"I know. Can I go to sleep now, please?"

"You know she does that—grabbing on to a man, blasting the movie-star smiles. It's all part of her game, and it does nothing for me."

Her game. Brenna was sick to the core of the damn game. "Why are we talking about this?"

"Because you're pissed at me, and I can tell you're pissed at me even though you keep trying to pretend you're not."

"I'm tired. I want to go to sleep. Can we just table this crap for tonight?"

A silence from him, a silence drawn tight as a wire. "Sure."

"Great. 'Night, then." With a loud sigh, she turned her back to him and closed her eyes.

Trav lay wide-awake in the dark for a long time. What the hell was the matter with her, anyway? How was he responsible for the tricks Summer pulled? Bren knew that Summer's behavior was in no way his fault. But still, Bren was mad at him.

Even if she wouldn't admit it outright.

He hated that she was mad at him. It made him feel out of sorts and angry right back, and edgy. Way edgy. Like he had ants crawling under his skin.

This whole thing was hard enough, being so close to her, knowing he couldn't reach for her. Not in the dark. Not when they were alone, just the two of them, and she smelled of apple-scented shampoo, so close he could reach out and gather her to him.

He could steal all the kisses he wanted when the cameras were watching, but not when they were alone. Because it wouldn't be right and he only had one out-of-date condom—and yeah, he now knew for a fact that the condom was out of date. Because even though he'd made it clear that they wouldn't be going there, he'd checked his wallet just to be sure. That condom had been ready for the trash two months ago.

Not that it mattered. He was never making love to her anyway, as he reminded himself at least a hundred times a night.

He turned on his side with his back to her, punched at the wadded-up T-shirt he was using as a pillow and shut his eyes good and tight.

The rules changed again the next day.

They stood outside the canteen as always, and Jasper laid out the new rules. "As I explained yesterday, today you will be judged and given points toward the next win and elimination. However, as an extra incentive to excellence, your day's work will also be a mini challenge. The winner today gets a night for two at the lodge. You'll stay in the Big Sky suite, finest suite in the house, *and* you'll share a gourmet dinner for two in the dining room.

"Each team will get four separate challenges. Teams will have until exactly 4:00 p.m. to tackle and complete these tasks. You will each be judged separately on how much you accomplish and how well you do each job, but you still have to work together to finish each task before moving on to the next one."

"If I win, do I get to choose who goes to the lodge with me?" Summer asked way too sweetly.

Jasper tipped his big black hat to her. "You do indeed."

"Wonderful." She flicked a flirty glance at Trav, followed by an evil grin at Brenna.

Oh, please. Brenna met those green eyes directly and refused to be baited.

This time, they drew their work partners and their job assignments from Jasper's hat. Brenna drew first. She unfolded the scrap of paper and read her new partner's name out loud. "Summer Knight."

Total setup. Just Roger and the writers, creating opportunities for sparks to fly. Brenna reminded herself that nobody had promised her this would be fair.

Summer stepped to her side and offered her hand. "Hey, partner."

Brenna made herself take it. "A pleasure to be working with you." She half expected lightning to strike her dead on the spot for telling such a whopping lie.

Trav drew next. He got Roberta. Steve drew Wally's name. And Fred ended up partnered with his son Rob.

Next, the partners drew the work assignments. Rusty

Boles offered Summer his upturned hat, and she drew out a folded slip of paper. Opening it, she read, "'One: clear mud and debris out of the east section of the west pasture ditch. Two: paint the exterior of the tool shed behind the blue barn. Three: paint the interior of same. Fourth challenge TBD as needed.'"

Brenna said, "I'm guessing there's some doubt we'll make it to the fourth task."

Summer sent her a mean little glare. "I am winnin' that night at the lodge, so don't you dare be a slacker."

Brenna considered how satisfying it would be to slap the woman silly, but she settled for a saccharine smile and said, "You certainly are motivated. I like that in a partner. If only you weren't so badly brought up, I'm thinking you and me would get along just fine."

Summer gasped. The whole group seemed to freeze in place, waiting for the fight to start.

Trav opened his mouth to speak, but Brenna shot him a glare and he kept quiet. She turned back to Summer and stared the blonde square in the eye. *Bring it on.*

But Summer turned to Jasper. "Can we get going? We've only got till four."

So Brenna wouldn't be taking Summer down this morning, after all. She couldn't decide whether she felt relieved or disappointed.

Jasper called Roberta, Wally and Rob forward. They drew the tasks for their teams.

Then Jasper announced, "Necessary tools and equipment are ready at the task sites. A task is not considered finished until you clean up after yourselves, which means returning all equipment and checking it in here at the canteen. Good luck, everyone." He pulled a pistol from the holster at his hip and aimed it skyward. "Ready, set…go!" The shot rang out.

They all took off running, each team in a different direction, followed by a scattering of cameramen and Anthony's assistants. Brenna and Summer beat feet to the west, jumping a pasture fence to get to the assigned ditch, where a wrangler waited with shovels, hoes and work gloves.

Summer pointed. "You start from that end and I'll start back there." She aimed her thumb over her shoulder. "We'll meet in the middle."

Seemed like a good plan to Brenna. Unless one of them came up against some obstruction too big to handle alone, they wouldn't even have to be near each other for most of the job. "Works for me." She took a pair of gloves, a shovel and a hoe and headed to her end.

Brenna worked hard and fast. She kind of hated to admit it, but Summer did, too. A couple of sweaty, dirty hours later, they had that ditch running again. Covered in mud and not even caring, they grabbed their tools and made for the canteen, where a wrangler logged in the equipment.

As soon as that was done, Brenna and Summer whirled and raced for the shed behind the blue barn. The wrangler waiting there had cans of blue paint, brushes, drop cloths, rags and a couple of lightweight ladders.

Thank God the shed wasn't that big. Even better, it was already scraped and primed. And there wasn't a separate trim color. Everything would be blue, including the door on the south wall.

Too bad they had to use brushes. That would take longer than spraying or rolling—not that Brenna's opinion of how best to do the job meant squat to anyone at this point.

They each took a wall and got going.

Three hours passed before the lunch bell rang.

Covered in mud from the first challenge and dotted with spatters of blue paint, Summer peeked around the corner of the shed. "You hungry?"

Brenna wiped a drip of paint off the end of her nose with the back of her hand. "Hell, no."

They painted through lunch. When the shed was covered in fresh blue paint, Brenna asked the wrangler, "Won't we need all this stuff to paint the inside?"

"Doesn't matter. It's part of the task to check in the equipment at the end of each job."

She considered calling the guy a few bad names, but she didn't want to waste the energy it would take. She and Summer slammed the lids back on the paint cans, grabbed everything but the ladders and made for the canteen.

The wrangler there reminded them that they needed to bring in the ladders, too. They raced for the shed, shouldered the ladders and hauled them back to the canteen.

Finally the wrangler checked them in—and then hit them with the news that they would need those ladders for the interior of the shed. "You can go ahead and take them back with you."

Summer made a growling sound. "There is crap and there is crap. And *this* is crap."

"Totally," muttered Brenna. She didn't like Summer, but the rodeo star spoke the truth, and Brenna felt honor bound to register solidarity on the issue of crap.

"Take 'em or don't," replied the wrangler. "It's up to you."

What could they do? They needed the ladders, even if they had to haul them back and forth across a pasture for no apparent reason other than to piss them off, wear them out and make them suffer. Because that made good drama. And reality TV was all about good drama.

Shouldering the ladders, they trudged to the shed. The wrangler was waiting for them inside with equipment identical to what they'd used on the exterior. Except that the paint was white.

Brenna looked on the bright side. At least the guy offered them bottled water.

They drank the water and got to work.

An hour or so later, the chuck wagon bell rang for a mini challenge.

Summer asked, "You going?"

"And win what? A camp pillow? No, thanks."

They kept painting until the interior of the shed was white. Again, it took two trips to the canteen to get everything turned in.

Spurs jingled as Jasper entered the canteen, a cameraman close on his heels. "Congratulations, ladies. It's five after three, and you've completed three tasks out of four." He gave them each a bottle of water. "Drink up, because you need to stay hydrated." As they guzzled the water, he continued, "And now for your fourth and final challenge…"

First, Jasper magnanimously announced that, due to the distance between the canteen and their final challenge, this time they would not be required to turn in their equipment, which consisted of a length of rope for each of them.

Outside, a pickup waited. They jumped in the back for a bouncy ride to their destination. A wrangler and a couple of cameramen went with them, filming them through the fifteen-minute trip.

Summer was a mess, spattered with mud, blue and white paint speckling her hair. Brenna knew she looked no better.

They stopped for the wrangler to jump out and open a gate, and then they were off across the pasture. Cows and their calves lifted their heads from the grass, ears twitching as they watched the truck go by. They crested a rise, and she spotted the crew below them on the bank of a muddy pond. One of Anthony's assistants and more cameras were waiting there to shoot their fourth challenge.

The pickup pulled to a stop. "Let's go," said the wrangler.

They all jumped down from the bed.

In the middle of the pond, on a small, soggy-looking scrub-grass island, two cows and their calves huddled, bawling unhappily. The muddy wranglers watching from the water's edge must have dragged the poor critters out there. And for the fourth challenge, it was Brenna and Summer's job to get them all safely back to dry land.

The sound guys stole several minutes of their time wrapping their body mic transmitters in plastic bags and taping the microphones behind their ears. "Try to keep your heads above water," one of them suggested.

Both Brenna and Summer laughed at that one.

"It's three thirty," announced the assistant director. "You have half an hour, ladies."

They looped their ropes around their necks and under one arm and waded in.

Their boots made sucking sounds in the muddy bottom as they slogged toward the island. Twenty feet from the bank, the bottom fell out from under them as the pond got too deep to stand. Brenna's boots dragged on her, but it wasn't too bad.

They were still a good two hundred feet away from the island—way too far to swim back to the shallows and use their ropes. Plus, roping presented some other problems. Calves followed their mamas, so they would need to rope the cows. No way could Brenna pull thirteen hundred pounds of unwilling beef into the pond.

That left plan B. Treading water, Brenna suggested, "We could swim around behind them."

Summer thought that over. "Nobody said we *had* to use the ropes."

"Exactly." Contrary to popular belief, cattle were smart, social creatures. They could swim just fine—when provided with the proper motivation. "But one of them could be a kicker," Brenna warned.

Summer grunted. "Time's running out. I say we take our chances."

"Okay, then. Let's do it."

Brenna went left; Summer went right. They swam around the island and climbed out behind the animals, who turned their heads to eye them with suspicion. Brenna moved toward one cow, while Summer advanced on the other one.

It only took a couple of well-timed smacks on the rump to get the mamas moving. Neither of them kicked, thank God. The cows bawled in annoyance, but they got in the water, their calves following close behind.

Piece of cake. The animals swam straight for the cameras. Summer and Brenna slid into the pond after them and swam for shore behind them. Both cows and one calf made it all the way to the bank without incident.

The second calf got stuck trying to get his footing when he reached the shallows. All it took was Brenna's boost on his bony behind and he was up and staggering toward his mama on the bank. He made it, too.

Brenna stood in a foot and a half of water, soaking wet with a soggy rope around her neck. Her hands braced on her hips, she called to the crew on the bank. "Did we make it in time?"

The assistant director gave her a thumbs-up.

She let out a whoop of triumph—right before Summer shoved her hard from behind.

Chapter Ten

Brenna's whoop turned to a startled cry. She staggered forward, barely saving herself from a face-plant in pond water. Whirling on the other woman, she flipped her wet braid back over her shoulder and demanded, "What the hell, Summer?"

Summer only stepped up—and shoved her backward, hard, with both hands.

Brenna went down, sprawling backward, the water closing over her— until she got her feet under her and popped upright again. She pushed at the constraining rope, getting it up and over her head, tossing it away from her as she sputtered, "What is the *matter* with you?"

Summer didn't answer. She tossed her rope off, too. And then she waded right up close to Brenna again and drew her arm back.

As Summer's open palm swung toward her, Brenna

realized that she was about to get bitch slapped and no one on the bank was going to do a thing to stop it. The cameras were still rolling.

Because a girl fight was exactly the kind of thing they loved on reality TV.

Brenna brought up her arm just in time to block Summer's blow, simultaneously reaching under with her free hand to shove the blonde in the chest. Summer windmilled her arms. With a screech, she toppled over on her butt. Muddy water went flying as Summer started to stand up.

Back in high school, Brenna's wild friend Leonie was constantly getting in fights. Leonie always said that once the other girl went down, your best bet was to make sure she didn't get up until she'd surrendered.

With a muttered, "No, you don't," Brenna jumped on Summer.

They rolled around in the shallows, hitting and slapping, pulling each other's hair, one going under, then rising, taking the upper hand and pushing the other beneath the surface. Summer was relentless.

But Brenna was bound and determined to end up the winner. And at last she did. Grabbing Summer by one wrist, she twisted the blonde's arm up hard against the small of her back. Summer gave a strangled-sounding moan.

"Up. Now." Brenna rose, pulling Summer with her. "Had enough?" she whispered in the other woman's ear.

"God, I really hate you!" Summer cried. "You're everybody's sweetheart, and it makes me want to puke."

Brenna almost laughed. All her life, she'd been the wild one, the one who inevitably managed to get herself in trouble. But somehow, on *The Great Roundup*, she got to be the sweet one. She clucked her tongue at Summer. "And here I kind of thought we were finally getting along."

Summer gave a smug little snort. "Fooled you, didn't I?"

From the bank, the assistant director signaled them forward.

Brenna commanded, "Start walking. Do not stop until we're both on dry land."

Summer and Brenna, dripping wet from head to toe, did a pair of OTFs right there on the edge of the pond. Summer acted like she'd won the fight, announcing that it was about time Little Miss Perfect ended up on her ass in a mucky pond.

Brenna played it breezy, smiling at the camera, waving her hand. "What can I tell you? Girls will be girls."

Once the interviews were done, crew and cast alike went directly to the canteen, where everyone else was waiting.

Trav took one look at Brenna and demanded, "What happened?"

"You should see the other girl." She flipped out a hand toward Summer several feet away.

"Whoa." He reached for her, pulling her close against his side.

As always, his touch, his very nearness, felt way too good. "Trav! You'll get mud and paint all over you."

He nuzzled her wet, filthy hair. "You're cute when you're dirty. And come on. Tell me what happened."

"Summer started a fight with me."

"But did *you* finish it?"

"Oh, you'd better believe I did."

"That's my girl."

My girl. She liked the sound of that way too much.

Jasper called for attention. The host gave a shorter-than-usual speech about which team had taken on what challenges. The judges sang a song and then the winner of the night at the lodge was announced.

The judge with the smallest hat said, "Brenna O'Reilly, step forward."

She couldn't believe it. She'd scored the highest of all of them, points that would go to keep her safe from elimination when this ongoing challenge ended. Best of all, she'd won the night at the lodge.

The judge gingerly patted her dirty shoulder and explained that she'd won because she and Summer, as a team, had been fast, focused and resourceful. They were one of two teams, with Trav and Roberta, who'd finished all four tasks.

But Brenna had made the highest score of all, digging out the ditch a little faster, painting that shed a little more expertly and coming up with the best way to get two cows and their bawling babies across a pond and back to dry land. The judge didn't mention the fight. But Brenna did kind of wonder how many points Summer had lost for starting a fight she didn't even manage to win.

Well, too bad for Summer. The rodeo star had gotten exactly what she deserved—a whupping. Brenna's mom would not be happy with her when the fight aired on national TV, but Brenna refused to feel bad for holding her own.

"Now, Brenna." Jasper wiggled his black eyebrows at her. "Who will you take with you for your luxury night at the lodge?"

Her gaze just naturally went to Trav. He looked so proud for her. She felt a delicious little flutter of anticipation under her breastbone. A night in a luxury suite with Trav. It sounded so tempting.

But it wasn't, not really. Because nothing would happen between them. All their hot, sexy loving was the fake kind, just for the cameras.

Ugh. She'd almost rather choose Roberta. They could order up some food, give each other mani-pedis and watch romantic movies.

But Trav was her partner in this big adventure, and she had her role as his adoring fiancée to play. They all needed to believe that she couldn't wait to be alone in a big bed with the man who owned her heart and made her body beg for more.

She asked, "Travis, will you spend a night at the lodge with me?"

He stepped forward and took her outstretched hand.

Jasper gestured grandly at the white van that waited to take them to the lodge.

The Big Sky suite was perfection, with a fancy sitting room and a giant bedroom, including a wonderful king-size bed with a carved headboard and pillows for days. Both rooms had huge windows looking out on mountain views crowned by wide slices of endless blue sky.

Their suitcases, which they hadn't seen for weeks now, waited in the bedroom, packed full of lovely clean clothes. Gerry had them change into flip-flops and took their dirty boots and socks to be cleaned.

Once they'd had a tour of the suite, they got to hand

over their body mics. The camera crew and director left them to clean up for dinner.

Alone at last, they stood in the middle of the sitting room, staring at each other.

"I can't believe we're here," she whispered—more in awe than in fear that there might be recording devices stashed nearby. There probably were, but she'd grown way too accustomed to all that by now.

Brenna pointed over her shoulder in the general direction of the gorgeous bathroom with its walk-in shower, jetted tub and twin sinks. "You go first, but make it fast. I want some quality time in that tub."

He grabbed the remote and turned on the big TV over the fireplace—at full volume.

She winced at the sound. "Trav!"

He waved her close and put his lips against her mud-spattered ear. "Check for cameras and recorders while I clean up."

She nodded and then yelled, "Turn it down!" just in case anyone was listening.

"Sorry." He punched the power button, dropped the remote on the coffee table and headed for the bathroom.

Brenna checked the living room first. She peered in every nook and cranny, looking for hidden cameras and tiny, nearly invisible microphones. She found none, but that didn't mean they weren't there.

She kept looking. In the bedroom, she pulled open the drawer of one of the twin nightstands—and found condoms of every size, flavor, style and color.

Brenna threw back her head and laughed. Apparently, Real Deal Entertainment wanted their contestants to practice safe sex.

A few minutes later, Trav emerged from the bathroom in a navy blue shirt, new jeans and dress boots. He looked so good and smelled all woodsy and clean. She felt a sharp tug of longing down inside her. Really, he was way too hot and handsome. It so wasn't fair.

His eyes asked, *Find anything?* She grinned, thinking about the drawer full of condoms. "What?" he demanded.

Let him find them himself.

She shook her head and headed for the bath.

Her shower took longer than she would have liked. The paint in her hair was especially stubborn.

Finally, she got all the paint off and sank into that beautiful tub. She soaked for an hour, then took her sweet time getting dressed for dinner.

Eventually, Travis tapped on the door. "Brenna, you okay?"

Leaning close to the mirror, she stroked mascara on her upper lashes. "Just a minute…"

"They're at the door, ready to take us to the dining room."

"Coming." She smoothed on cherry lip gloss and then stood back to check herself out in the mirror. "Not bad."

"Bren, we need to —" He blinked as she pulled open the door. And then his eyes went low and lazy.

Her heart leaped at that hot, hungry look on his face. Yeah, he kept insisting that he wouldn't make love to her. But right at that moment, she truly believed he wanted to.

He gave a low whistle. "Wow." She preened a little in her red dress that skimmed her curves just right and ended a few inches above her knees. He reached out and stroked a hand down her hair. "Straight and sleek again."

"Trav…"

He eased his hand up under her hair and wrapped it around the nape of her neck. Those rough, warm fingers felt so good against her skin, as though she'd been born to feel his touch. "So beautiful." He tried to pull her in for a kiss.

She resisted, dipping out from under his touch and asking, "Find anything…interesting?" Meaning cameras or microphones.

"Nothing," he replied.

She couldn't hold back a chuckle. "Did you happen to look in the drawer by the bed?"

He stifled a snort of laughter. "Oh, yeah." And then he leaned close again.

She didn't back away that time. He was so hard to resist. And judging by the blue fire in his eyes, he really did want to kiss her.

With a tiny smile, she let him reel her in. His warm lips brushed hers, and his neat beard tickled her just enough to send an eager shiver across her skin.

And then came the knock on the outer door.

Trav let her go with clear reluctance. "Dinner's waiting."

The table for two was in a private nook, with a white tablecloth, a floating candle, a rose in a crystal vase and the lodge's best china and silver. The perfect setting for romance. Over delicious food and a nice bottle of wine, they held hands across the table, now and then bending close to share more than one lingering kiss. He told her how much he loved her, and she said it right back to him.

But it was all for the cameras now that they were mic'd up again.

Travis didn't know that in her case it was true—and she wasn't going to tell him, not until they were back home again living in the real world. Maybe not even then.

Who could say what would happen? They needed to win a million bucks together. And then they could talk about what might happen next.

Oh, but she did love him, so much, more than anything. Her love felt all bottled up inside her sometimes, pushing at her rib cage, aching to bust out. She wouldn't let it, though, not now, not till all this was over. Maybe.

Or maybe not.

But the uncertain future aside, oh, she longed to be his lover for real—just the two of them in a room alone, with nobody watching. Brenna and Travis, doing whatever came naturally.

Even if she couldn't profess her love from the heart, she could have that, at least. And tonight was her best chance. Upstairs they had a real bed with actual sheets and piles of fat pillows. If ever a setting was made for seduction, the Big Sky suite was it.

And she was bold Brenna O'Reilly, the one who took chances. The one who stood tall, threw caution to the wind and went after what she wanted.

It was getting dark when Gerry ushered them back upstairs. The crew hung around to film them sharing steamy kisses at the door to the suite.

And then, finally, they got to take off their mics. A minute later, they were inside, with not a crew member in sight.

She turned the privacy lock and leaned back against the door with a long, happy sigh. "I thought they'd never leave us alone."

His blue eyes gleamed at her. She knew he wanted to kiss her again. He stepped in close. "I shouldn't..."

"Oh, yeah. You should." She lifted her mouth, offering it to him.

And he took it—leaning in, covering her lips with his, kissing her long and slow and deep.

She reached out, slid her hungry arms around his lean waist and gathered him into her, moaning when she felt him growing hard against her belly.

He pulled away too fast and looked down at her, eyes blazing, face flushed. "We have to watch it."

"Shut. Up." And she yanked him back to her again.

They kissed for the longest time, standing there against the door. His hands cradled her face, drifted down her arms and then back up again.

For the first time ever, he cupped her breasts. She melted inside and moaned against his mouth.

He pulled back, but then he leaned close again to whisper, "You know it's gotta be a setup, right? The big bed, the drawer of condoms?"

"Trav." She bit his earlobe. "Look at it this way. When are we going to get another chance like this?"

He kissed her again, a kiss that made her knees wobble and her heart dance. "You're sure?"

She felt a slow grin tip the corners of her mouth. "That was way too easy."

He leaned close once more and pressed his forehead to hers. He seemed to be trying really hard to control his breathing. "I can't stand it anymore, Bren. I want you too damn much."

"Exactly the words I've been longing to hear."

"You're sure?"

She pressed her cheek to his and whispered, "The answer is still yes. You can stop asking now."

He nuzzled her ear. "Even if the room was clean before, they could have put cameras in here while we were downstairs."

"So be it. How much can they show, anyway? It's prime-time network TV."

But he was insistent. "One more sweep. It can't hurt."

Reluctantly, they let go of each other to check the whole suite again.

Finally, she threw up her hands. "Nothing. Can we give it up now, please?"

"We can't be a hundred percent certain they're not filming us. And even if what they get doesn't end up on the show, it could turn up somewhere else. You realize that, right?"

"Trav, I have to tell you. At this point, I don't even care."

Travis loved that she wanted him enough to be reckless. But what would happen tonight was just between the two of them and he meant to keep it that way. "It won't kill us to be cautious."

Brenna groaned and glared up at him. "Travis Dalton, don't you tell me that you've changed your mind again."

He caught her stubborn chin. "Not a chance." He wanted her too much. More than any of the too many women he'd known. More than the win. More than his share of the prize money that would build him his own house and give him a real say on the family ranch.

Travis lowered his head and kissed her. She tasted so good, like heaven, with a hint of coffee and chocolate from dessert.

"You've got too many clothes on," she accused when he finally lifted his head.

He chuckled. "We'll get to that." And then he bent close again and whispered to her, explaining what they needed to do. "First, let's turn off all the lights…"

Once the lights were out, he closed the curtains in the bedroom. Faint light bled in from the big windows in the sitting area, just enough that they could move around without bumping into the furniture.

He took her hand and led her through the shadows to the side of the bed. They undressed each other slowly, punctuating the process with endless, tender kisses. When they were down to their underwear, he pulled back the covers. She got in, grabbing his hand and pulling him in after her. He settled the blankets over them before he reached for her.

She went into his arms eagerly, with a long, happy sigh. It felt so good to hold her. She curved into him, fitting just right, as though she was born to be there.

He cradled her close, his arms tight around her, her head tucked under his chin. It had been way too long since he'd held her like this—since the night in the lean-to at the high meadow. They'd had to sleep close that night to stay warm.

He pressed his lips to her silky hair and whispered, "Remember that night in the high meadow?"

Her lips brushed his throat. "Mmm-hmm. It was so cold. And I was so grateful to have you all wrapped around me."

He confessed, "I resented the morning when it came."

"Why?"

"Because I knew we were going back down the mountain and I might not get another chance to hold you all night long."

She tipped her head back and kissed him under the chin. "Travis Dalton, you are the sweetest man."

"Sweet?" He ran a finger down her slim, strong arm and loved the way her breath caught when he did it. "Are you kidding? I'm the one with the wild streak and the troublemaking ways, remember?"

"I thought that was me—and anyway, if you *are* a troublemaker, you're *my* troublemaker, at least for tonight, and don't you forget it."

He kissed the end of her nose. "And you are mine."

"Yes," she said, her whisper slightly breathless now. "All yours." She caught his hand and placed it on her breast, which was firm and pliant—perfect, even through the lace of her bra.

Now he was the one sucking in a sharp breath. "Brenna." He found her nipple under the lace and teased it a little.

Her hungry little gasp sent a bolt of hot desire shooting through him.

All these years and years he'd known her. Never had he dared to believe they would ever get here. In a big bed, just the two of them, with only a few scraps of fabric between them. He had never let himself even *think* about making love to her—well, not until lately. And now he couldn't *stop* thinking about it.

She amazed him, always had. And even more since he'd spent the past four and a half weeks with her. Not only was she the prettiest girl in Montana, she had imagination and resourcefulness, a great sense of humor, and the willingness to stay the course no matter how tough the task.

And she was kind. Generous, too.

"What *are* you thinking, Travis?" Her eyes shone up at him through the darkness.

"Good things."

"About?"

"You." He dipped his thumb under the lacy cup that covered her breast, tugging it down, freeing her softness to his waiting hand. "So beautiful." He lowered his head and captured her nipple, rolling it on his tongue, giving it a little nip with his teeth.

"Travis!" she gasped.

"Um?"

And she sighed. "Do that some more."

He pulled the sheet up and over their heads.

She laughed then, muffling the sound by pressing her face against his chest. "I feel like a naughty kid in a fort of blankets."

He kissed her hair, her cheek, the silky skin of her throat. "Works for me."

She stroked a hand, fingers spread, down his chest to his belly. And lower. He had to hold back a groan as she touched him through his boxer briefs. He was rock hard already, and they'd hardly begun.

"Let's take off the rest," she whispered in his ear.

"You're on." He let his fingers wander over the smooth flesh that covered her rib cage, all the way to her back and the clasp of her bra. A flick of his fingers and he had it unhooked.

She made a sweet, humming sound and did the rest, slipping the straps down her arms, pulling it off, lifting the blanket on her side just enough to drop it to the rug.

He slipped his fingers under the elastic of her panties. "Let me."

"Oh, yes!"

"Lift up." And she lifted. He took those panties off and away.

"Now these," she commanded, her cool, clever fingers on the waistband of his boxer briefs. He didn't argue. She eased the elastic over his erection. He took it from there, whipping them down and off, sticking his arm out from under the covers to toss them away.

And that was it. They were completely naked under the covers. Clasping the sleek curve of her shoulder, he pulled her into him. They lay on their sides, face-to-face.

She offered up her mouth, and he took it in one of those kisses that sent him straight to paradise. He dipped his tongue in and caressed all the wet, slick surfaces beyond her parted lips.

As he kissed her, he let his hands wander to the places he'd never dared to go before—the bare curve of her waist, the firm slope of her hip, the round, high globes of her gorgeous bottom, the strong, smooth length of her thigh.

No, he couldn't see her, not clearly. She was a sweet, soft shadow in this secret cave beneath the blankets with him. He wished he might feast his eyes on the sight of her.

But in the end, it didn't really matter.

He saw her in a deeper way. She was burned into his brain and branded on his heart.

And what he couldn't worship with his eyes right now, he would memorize forever by touching her everywhere. He cradled her breasts, kissing one and then the other. They fit his hands just right, her nipples tight and hard, pressing so perfectly into the center of his palm.

She whispered his name as he stuck out his tongue to taste the valley of sweet flesh between her breasts. He followed that valley down, rolling her to her back so he could rise over her and trail his hungry lips down into the hollow of her waist.

He dipped his tongue in her navel, nipped the softness just below it. She quivered beneath him, reaching for him, weaving her fingers into his hair, murmuring breathless encouragements as he kissed his way lower still.

Sliding a hand down the top of her thigh, dipping it under to hook the back of her knee, he eased her leg up so that he could slip under it, coming up in the place he most longed to be.

He kissed her, a rain of kisses, really. He scattered them across her belly and downward. She moaned when he nuzzled her, parting her, blowing out a slow breath on her wet, waiting core.

She smelled of flowers, of honey. She tasted so sweet, musky and womanly. He gave himself up to the taste and the feel of her, using his hungry mouth and his fingers, too, driving her higher, until she was whimpering, tugging at his shoulders, trying to pull him up into her arms.

Not yet...

He kept kissing her, caressing her, dipping one finger and then two into her wet heat, stroking her.

He knew the moment she couldn't hold out against him any longer. He felt her go over, and he smiled against her secret flesh as her climax rolled through her. She called out his name and he had to reach up, cover her mouth with his hand to help her hold back her breathless, excited cries.

Not until she finally went loose and boneless, the pulsing of her climax fading to a flutter, did he sweep up her body to press his lips to hers.

She grabbed for him, her fingers digging into his shoulders at first, a long sigh escaping her. And then she wrapped her arms so tight around him, kissing him back with sweet heat and hungry tenderness. Those eager hands of hers strayed down over his back, grabbing on tight and yanking him hard and close.

Now he was the one moaning, as her knowing fingers slipped between them and wrapped around the aching length of him, tight and demanding, just the way he liked it. She stroked him, long, strong strokes, running her thumb up over the flare, rubbing the head, until he was sure he would lose it right then and there.

But somehow, he held back, kept himself hovering just on the brink for an eternity of pleasure as she kissed him and played him with her sweet, clutching hand.

"You make me crazy." She breathed the words against his open mouth.

A laugh that was more like a groan escaped him. "*I* make *you* crazy? I might have a heart attack right here and now."

"It's not any more than what you just did to me."

"You're killing me." The whispered words came out of him sounding like a plea.

Her naughty hand moved up, over, down. "I want you to feel me, Trav. Every stroke, every kiss."

"I do, I swear to you. Bren, you know I do."

"I want you to remember this, remember *us*."

"I could never forget."

"I want…everything, Travis. For as long as this crazy ride lasts. I want all there is. With you."

"Yes." He really had no idea what he was agreeing to. Only that somehow, he had to make her understand that she was something special, that there was no one like her. "You have it. You…always did. You have to know that's true."

"Oh, Travis…" And she kissed him, another endless, seeking kiss as she continued to stroke him fast and hard and so, so good.

"I can't— We have to— Right now," he babbled low against her parted lips.

How she understood his meaning, he would never know. But she did. "The drawer!" she cried in a torn little whisper. She loosened her grip on him enough that he could lift up and reach out from under their tent of blankets.

He got hold of the drawer pull and gave it a tug. Then he dipped his hand in and took out a condom. He had no idea what kind it was. Ribbed, flavored, purple, bright green? He felt around the rim—no weird spikes or anything.

"Got it?" she panted, her whisper sweet and urgent.

"Yeah." He retreated back under the blankets again.

"Oh, please let me," she begged, eager and earnest and downright adorable. He gave her the pouch. "Roll over," she commanded, suddenly bossy.

Grinning, though he ached with the need to have her immediately, he stretched out on his back. A moment later, she held him steady as she rolled the condom down over him, snugging it in at the base with great care.

And then, before he could grab her and roll her under

him, she hitched a leg over him, taking him firmly in hand and guiding him to the brink of her sweet, waiting heat.

He groaned way too loud. How could he help it?

"Shh." She sat up tall on him, bending only enough to press a finger against his lips. "We're being quiet, remember?"

He answered with a tortured sound. It was the best he could do as she slowly took him into her.

Slowly, so very slowly, she came down on him. He reached for her, taking her hips between his two hands, steadying both of them as her body accepted him.

It was glorious. *She* was glorious, so wet and hot and tight—and so giving, too.

Always, he thought.

Always and forever. The words got stuck in his mind, echoing softly. He wasn't sure why. But they seemed like the right words.

Yeah, he'd been with way too many women. But there was only one Brenna. Her body felt just right to him, thrilling and perfect and also familiar. Like he'd been lost for the longest time and finally sighted the lights of home.

Found. He was found. Finally, with her.

She surrounded him, claiming him, until he couldn't take the wonderful agony of it. With a final sharp tug, he pulled her all the way down.

"Oh!" And then she let out a long sigh. "Oh, yes..." For a moment, neither of them moved a muscle. They absorbed the reality—that she held him within her.

All the way in.

And then, with a soft moan of surrender, she curved her body over him. Her sweet-scented hair fell along his shoulder, a big swatch of it slipping, like a whisper of silk, down the side of his neck.

Her tender breasts felt so good against the hard wall of his chest. He reached up and wrapped his hand around her nape, guiding her mouth down to meet his in a wet, open kiss.

And then they were moving, rocking together, urgent and hungry, then slow, deep and hard. But the kiss never broke. They kept their mouths fused together. She breathed in his yearning sighs, and he swallowed her moans.

He rolled so he had the top position and then rolled again. Now they lay on their sides.

She was all around him, scent and sweetness, spice and heat. He hadn't known, had never realized that sex could be like this. So true and simple, so deep and tender and right. She'd probably gone and ruined him for any other woman.

Well, so what?

He was finally ready and willing to be ruined. He could lie here with her, buried in blankets, rolling and rocking, straight through to the day after the end of forever.

Too bad this rough, hot magic couldn't last. He felt the end coming. There was no way to stop it.

He rolled again, striving to hold the last shreds of his control. She was under him, her mouth fused to his, her hands clutching his back, rocking him to paradise.

And then he felt her go over. He drank in her keening cry as her body pulsed around him.

That did it. His climax roared through him, mowing him down, dragging him under.

He let out a shout.

"Shh, Trav. Shh…" Her hand was there, covering his mouth. He chanted her name against her palm as the world turned inside out.

Chapter Eleven

Some idiot knocked on the suite's door at five the next morning.

Travis put his arm across his eyes and willed whoever it was to go away.

The knock came again.

He rolled to his side and kissed Brenna's bare shoulder. "Somebody's at the door."

"Mmm."

"I'll get it." He started to slide over the side of the bed.

But her hand shot out and closed on his wrist. "Get back here."

He put up zero resistance. She gave a tug and he rolled back to her, wrapping his other arm around her, drawing her close. She felt like paradise and she smelled of apples and sex. He wanted to spend the whole day in bed with her. But they had a million bucks to win.

Resignedly, he whispered, "It's Gerry. You know that, right?"

"Ugh." She tucked her head under his chin and wiggled a little, burrowing in.

He pressed a kiss into the wild tangle of her hair. "Gerry's not giving up."

She made more grumbly sounds and snuggled even closer.

The next knock was louder.

She bit his chest. Lightly. "Suddenly, I hate Gerry." With a sulky little moan, she pushed him away. "Go. Answer it."

He slid over to the edge of the bed again, sticking his head out from under the covers, spotting his jeans right there on the rug. Scooping them up, he dragged them under the sheet with him and pulled them on.

The knocking started up again.

"Hold on! I'm coming." He rose to his feet. "Stay there. I'll see if I can get rid of him."

"Ha. There is no getting rid of Gerry." She flipped the blankets over her head.

He laughed and shut the bedroom door behind him before answering the insistent knock. "Gerry. What a surprise." For once, the guy didn't have a camera crew with him. But there was a wrangler and a woman with a food trolley

"Rise and shine." Gerry handed Travis a pile of clothes as the wrangler stepped forward and set both his boots and Brenna's inside the door. "We couldn't get the paint out of Brenna's shirt and jeans. Tell her she can trade them for something from her suitcase."

"Will do." Travis stepped aside so the woman could

wheel in the trolley bearing a coffee service and two covered plates.

Gerry glanced at his watch. "In forty-nine minutes you both need to be fed, dressed and ready to go."

"All right."

"Requests? Complaints?"

He almost smiled as he remembered the night before. "Not a one."

"Well, all right then. See you at six." With a wave, Gerry, the wrangler and the girl from hospitality services headed off down the hall.

The bedroom door opened and there was Brenna in a terry-cloth robe with High Lonesome embroidered above the tempting curve of her left breast. "I smell coffee."

"Come and get it."

But she didn't. She just stood there in that white robe, her red hair sleep tangled on her shoulders, her cheeks pink with beard burn and her eyes full of promises he aimed to make her keep.

"Trav…"

"C'mere."

She ran to him. He wrapped his arms around her. She pressed those soft lips to the side of his throat and whispered, "All those condoms in that drawer?"

"Yeah?"

"You need to figure out a way we can take them back to camp with us when we go."

Brenna spent the ride back to the canteen trying not to look at Travis. She knew if she met his eyes, she would lose it, just burst out laughing. Partly from happiness. Because last night was the best night of her life.

But also because every pocket they had between them was stuffed with condoms. As were their boots and their underwear.

Gerry stopped the van near the canteen. "Report to Roger inside," he said.

"Sure will," replied Travis as he pushed his door open. "Thanks, Gerry."

"My pleasure. Toodle-oo."

Brenna slid across and followed Travis out. Taking their sweet time about it, they started for the entrance to the canteen, switching course as soon as Gerry drove off.

Laughing, they took off running for the tent village, where the others were finishing up breakfast. Steve called out a greeting. Roberta, sitting with him beside the campfire, signaled them over.

"Be right there!" Brenna called and ducked into their tent behind Travis.

Chortling like a couple of complete fools, they emptied their pockets, undid their clothes and pulled off their boots to shake out the contents. Then they scrambled to put it all out of sight.

Brenna smoothed her hair and checked to see that she had everything buttoned. Then she followed Travis out of the tent. She got welcome-back hugs from Roberta and Steve, and then she and Travis raced back to the canteen to report in to Roger.

That day she got paired with Wally on another series of short challenges. It all went off reasonably well.

But the best part was that night. She and Trav zipped their sleeping bags together and made love until midnight. She got to fall asleep in his arms and wake up with him spooning her.

The next day, the judges named a winner and a loser of the four days of random challenges. Steve got his immunity bracelet. Fred Franklin went to the lodge.

And Brenna got another beautiful night in Trav's arms.

Sunday, they started a two-day challenge. They lost Wally on Monday. And then they were six.

Tuesday, the Fourth of July, they gathered at the canteen bright and early to learn there would be no challenges that day in honor of the holiday. "Instead," Jasper announced, "each of you remaining contestants will have a visitor from home." On cue, a white van drove up. Travis's cousin Eli Dalton stepped out. And then Fallon.

With a happy cry, Brenna ran to meet her sister.

Fallon's arms went around her. "It's so good to see you."

Brenna hugged her tight. "I can't believe you're here." Then she whispered a warning, "Anything you say could end up on the show."

Her sister laughed. "I kind of thought so when they put this microphone in my hair— Oh, and I couldn't help but notice there are cameramen everywhere." She waved a hand in the direction of the cameras trained on them.

Brenna gave a shrug. "Hey. Welcome to *The Great Roundup.* Come on. Let's get out of here."

Brenna led the way down to the creek. They sat on the bank. "How are Jamie and the babies?"

"Perfect." Fallon stared out over the rushing water. "Katie tried to eat a spider yesterday."

"Yikes. Toddlers. Into everything."

"And Jamie's still looking for..." Fallon's voice

trailed off. "Oops." She pointed at the microphone tucked into her red curls. She didn't need to finish. Brenna understood. No need to share the Stockton family history with the world.

It was a sad story. Jamie and his siblings had been separated after the death of their parents almost twelve years ago. He and his sister Bella had been taken in by their grandparents. But Jamie's other sisters had been adopted out of state. Their older brothers, both over 18 at the time, went off on their own and hadn't come back. Jamie and Bella had found one of their sisters, Dana, in December. They were still searching for Luke, Daniel, Bailey and Liza. Brenna couldn't imagine how awful that must be, to lose the ones you loved and not know where to find them. But Jamie, Bella and Dana were doing all they could to reunite their family.

"Tell Jamie I'm…rooting for him," Brenna said lamely.

"You know I will." Fallon wrapped her arms around her knees and gave Brenna a long, slow once-over. "So. You're looking really good. And very happy."

"Love will do that to a girl." It was so easy to say now, because it was one hundred percent true. And ironically, she *could* say it in front of the cameras even though she'd never said it when it was just her and Travis alone.

Fallon's blue eyes were full of questions. "Bren, I can't help worrying."

"Don't."

"But are you sure?" She whispered the words, as though that would keep her body mic from picking them up.

"Positive. Certain beyond the last shadow of a fading doubt."

"But we both know Travis. What if he—"

"Fallon." Brenna shook her head. Whatever happened, she had a goal for her future and a job to do to make that future real. She was sticking with her plan, and her plan was to deal with any emotional fallout after the show wrapped. "I promise you, I love Travis and he makes me very happy."

"And I see that. You've got that special glow, but I still—"

"Please, Fallon. Let it be."

Fallon respected her request and didn't ask again.

Travis had taken his cousin Eli on a quick tour of the High Lonesome stables, with a camera crew trailing along behind. Back outside, they sat on the horse pasture fence to talk.

"Gotta admit," Travis said, "I was surprised to see *you* here." The oldest of his aunt Rita's boys, Eli was as steady and stalwart as they came, not the kind of guy to spend a day on location with a reality show.

Eli shrugged his big shoulders. "One of those producers and that casting director woman came out to the ranch to talk to me. They said they liked my look, whatever that means, and they asked me if I wanted to spend a day representing the family, visiting my cousin on *The Great Roundup*."

"And you agreed?" Travis shook his head.

"Don't look so amused. I can stand a little adventure. It's only one day."

"Maybe you need to consider getting on a show yourself."

Eli grunted. "This here, today, is it for me. I've got stock to move and hay to cut."

Overhead a hawk soared. The sky was powder blue dotted with fluffy white clouds. Travis stared off toward the mountains, thinking of Brenna, wondering what she and Fallon were up to.

"You're looking good," said Eli. "Kind of easy. Relaxed. Not so wild and crazy as before. It's working, huh?"

"Working?"

"With you and Brenna."

Travis wrapped both hands around the fence rail and looked his cousin steady in the eyes. "She's the best thing that's ever happened to me. I'm a very lucky man."

"Yeah," said Eli, nodding. "That's real love for you. I keep hoping that someday it'll happen for me."

Real love.

The hawk was only a black spot far in the distance now. Trav watched it vanish into the blue.

Real love.

Whatever this thing was with him and Bren, he was in it and in it deep.

No, he'd never been a forever type of guy. But Bren, she was different than any woman he'd ever known. She was special to him in a thousand different ways.

And sometimes lately he couldn't help dreaming of what it might be like if this thing they shared never had to end.

After the holiday break in the action, Jasper laid out a new challenge—with a twist. He announced that the immunity bracelets were being retired. From then on, everyone would be vulnerable to elimination at every challenge.

Two days later, on Friday, Summer got eliminated. The rodeo star had been quiet, subdued even, since Brenna had fought her and won the week before. Brenna almost felt sorry to see her go. The following Tuesday, Rob Franklin was let go.

The cast was shrinking fast. Only she and Trav, and Roberta and Steve were left.

That evening, Steve brought out the last bottle of Jack Daniel's left from the night of the chili challenge. After toasting all their fallen contestants, they lingered by the fire until almost midnight, reminiscing about what they'd been through to get this far.

And later, in their tent in the dark, Travis made love to Brenna slowly.

She whispered, "Make it last forever."

As he rose up above her she watched his eyes through the shadows, memorizing every whisper, every touch, every lingering kiss, so that no matter how it all ended up, she would have every moment she'd shared with him to keep in her heart forever.

The following morning at the canteen, Jasper announced that the next two days would be challenge-free. Steve and Roberta got time to themselves at the campsite, while Travis and Brenna were taken, along with a camera crew, to the lodge.

The van let them off in front of the lobby, where more cameras were waiting, along with a brunette in a short skirt and cowboy boots who introduced herself as "Lori Luckly, the world's premier cowboy wedding planner."

Brenna grabbed Travis's hand and held on tight. All

of a sudden, her heart was beating way too fast. Her cheeks burned, and her stomach felt like she'd swallowed a vat of acid. No one had mentioned the marriage clause for weeks. Brenna had begun to let herself believe that the wedding wasn't going to happen.

But the appearance of Lori Luckly proved otherwise.

It *was* happening. They were getting married on the show, pulling the ultimate fake-out in a world where everything real between people seemed to happen in whispers in the dark, where the cameras couldn't see and the microphones couldn't hear.

"This way, you two." Lori led them to a conference room inside the lodge.

Roger DelRay and a couple of the other production people were already there. As Brenna sat next to Travis, she didn't let go of his hand. No way. She clutched it like a lifeline.

The first order of business was whether or not to invite the families for the big day.

Lori said, "Of course, you'll both want your parents there. And your brothers and sisters."

Roger templed his fingers. "Definitely. We want that family feel, and that means we absolutely need the families there."

Brenna cleared her throat and croaked, "No."

Every head at that table swung her way.

She drew herself up. "Forget it. We don't want the families to come." Her mom and dad and Fallon and Fiona and her brothers did not need to be there to witness a marriage that was destined from the first "I do" to end in divorce. Neither did Trav's family, for that matter.

Roger had on his this-does-not-compute frown. "But

why not? Every woman wants Mom and Dad at her wedding."

Trav jumped to her rescue. "Roger, it's just not practical. We both have big families, and if you invite one family member, they're all going to want to come. That means a raft of confidentiality agreements from a bunch of people who have no skin in this game."

"Hmm," said Roger, rubbing his chin. "How many family members are we talking about, exactly?"

"Only counting parents, siblings and cousins?" Trav pretended to run numbers on his fingers. "Fifty, maybe? Sixty? Probably more."

"Hmm," Roger said again. Then he and the other producer put their heads together and conferred in whispers.

Trav kept after them. "Why don't we just bring back the rest of the cast for our big day? We're all like family now, anyway."

"Yeah!" Brenna piped up desperately. "That's what I want. I want Roberta for my maid of honor."

Trav chimed in with, "And Steve will be my best man."

The producers whispered to each other some more.

And finally, Roger nodded. "I like it. It'll be a family affair, after all. A family affair with your *Great Roundup* family."

Brenna almost felt like she could breathe again. She pasted on a giant smile. "Sounds perfect to me."

But it wasn't perfect.

Because it was actually happening. The only perfect thing about it was that at least her family *wouldn't* be there.

* * *

For the next three days, they had no challenges. *The Great Roundup* had gone wedding crazy. And Brenna and Travis were the stars of the show.

The professionals dressed them. They were filmed consulting with wardrobe people, trying on any number of possible wedding outfits, making their choices and then being fitted.

Brenna decided on a strapless marvel of satin and white lace—to be worn with her favorite purple boots. Trav chose a blue jacket and matching vest over a snowy-white shirt and a string tie. To keep it totally cowboy, he would wear jeans and boots. Roberta went for a short dress, chiffon and lace, in sunny yellow. Her boots were tan, tooled in white. And Steve got a vest and shirt like Trav's, but without the jacket. All the flowers would be daisies, yellow and white.

They scouted outdoor locations, riding around on horseback with a camera crew to film it all, checking out open fields and picturesque pastures.

In the end, they chose a spot not too far from the canteen, a wide, rolling field with the mountains in the distance. Jasper Ridge, it turned out, was an ordained minister. He would perform the ceremony.

The reception would be held outdoors, country-style, by the canteen. They would have barbecue for dinner, iced tea and champagne punch in mason jars—and a big white cake decked with frosting daisies.

After dinner, there would be dancing. Real Deal was bringing in a famous six-piece country band to provide music for the ceremony and the after-dinner dancing, too.

Bren and Trav worked with a choreographer on their

first dance, to "Wanted" by Hunter Hayes. Trav had picked the song, and Real Deal was trying to get permission to use the song on the show. If it didn't work out, she and Travis would have to redo the dance later to something Real Deal could get the rights to.

Brenna had tried to talk Trav into just dancing to something else. But he wouldn't budge.

"That song," he said, "reminds me of you." And that made her want to run away bawling. She was glad that he wanted her; she just wasn't ready to marry him.

Yet.

The whole process just felt so strange and disorienting. She prepared for her wedding in a daze. Somehow, through it all, she managed to keep her game face on.

They had to get a marriage license. Gerry and Lori Luckly took them to the county clerk's office. Nobody there seemed to recognize them, and they were in and out in no time. Still, to Brenna, getting that license was the worst.

All the rest of it—the dress, the dancing, the choice of location—just seemed like some weird, otherworldly fantasy. But the license brought it all home. Her fake engagement would culminate in a marriage that was all too real.

Through it all, Travis was wonderful. He stuck close to her, his hand wrapped around hers much of the time. She was so grateful for his strength and support, though she knew he wasn't any happier about it than she was. Yes, they were the bold ones in their families. But neither an O'Reilly nor a Dalton would ever get married unless they were deeply in love and planning on staying that way.

She tried to tell herself that what they were doing

wasn't *that* bad. Because she did love him, for real and true and probably forever. But her love couldn't really console her. They needed the time they weren't going to get, time for a real engagement, time to come to the choice of forever together.

Or not.

This wasn't about forever. This was about a million bucks, about winning the game.

And that made it cheap and wrong.

The night before the big event, in the privacy of their tent, Trav tried to get her to talk about it.

"Bren, come on. Look on the bright side."

"I'm trying. I am."

"We're so close. I'm betting that one of us will win the grand prize. Think about it. Look how far we've come."

"I know, Trav, you're right. We've done well."

"Damn straight. And you can't go checking out on me. We need to focus on making it all the way to the final challenge."

She reached up and pressed her palm to the side of his dear face. "I'm fine."

"You're lying."

She wrapped her arms around his neck and brought him down nose to nose with her. "I'm with you," she whispered. "You can count on me. I'm up for every challenge. Ready to give my all for the win."

"Bren." His warm breath brushed her lips. "It guts me to see you go freaked."

"I'm not freaked."

"You are. And beautiful, and so damn brave, trying so hard not to cave."

"Cave? Uh-uh. I'm not gonna cave, Trav."

"I know." His lips brushed hers. He tasted so good. Like everything precious and real and true. Like every great mystery she would never unravel.

She pulled him closer, needing him right then more than she ever had. Their lovemaking that night was so good, better than ever.

It didn't solve anything. But at least for a little while, she could forget everything but the feel of him within her, the strength in his arms around her. She focused on that, on the tender way he held her close to him. He swept her away to a place where there was only the two of them and she could pretend that what they had would never end.

Their wedding day dawned sunny and clear.

Brenna spent the morning at the lodge with Roberta. They were bathed, waxed and buffed within an inch of their lives, after which came the mani-pedis, and the professional hair and makeup, too.

While a pair of clever stylists did their hair side by side, Roberta suddenly reached out and clutched her arm. "I love him, Bren. I love Steve."

Brenna shifted a glance toward the ever-present camera crew. "Roberta," she warned softly.

Roberta threw up both hands. "So what? I love him, and I don't give a damn if the whole wide world knows it. I swear to God I never thought I would say that again. I swore I was through with love, that I would never in this lifetime trust my heart to another man. Wrong. Steve is it for me. The real thing. When the show's over, he's going back to his family's ranch in West Texas. He's sure I won't like it there. I don't know how to convince him to take me with him, that he's the one for me and I know it will work out for us."

Brenna leaned close to her friend. "Stop talking, start doing."

Roberta laughed. "What does that mean?"

"Follow him home."

"I don't— What if his family resents some woman more than ten years older than him moving in on him? What if *he* hates that I came?"

"What if *you* hate it? Either way, you need to find out, and the only way to find out is to go there."

"I know I won't hate it. I was raised on a ranch. If Steve's there, I'll be happy there."

"Well, then go there. It's all going to work out."

"You sound so sure."

"Roberta, I've seen you together. If that isn't love, I'll eat Jasper Ridge's ten gallon black hat."

It was such a beautiful setting—the open field with a pretty, rustic fence off in the background and the thick evergreen forest beyond that, and the mountains, shrouded in wisps of clouds, looming off in the distance.

The wedding guests in their Sunday best filled a set of bleachers. The whole cast was there, including Leah and Seth Stone. Leah looked beautiful in a sea-blue dress and Seth was already getting around on one crutch.

Brenna, sitting with Roberta in one of the white vans as they waited for the Wedding March to start, could see the Stones clearly through her side window. Leah glowed with happiness. Seth had his arm around her. As Brenna watched, Seth whispered in his wife's ear. Leah tipped her head back and laughed.

"Look at Seth and Leah," Roberta marveled. "I've never seen them so happy."

Brenna's throat felt tight, and her eyes burned. No doubt about it. Leah had found what she'd been longing for.

Across from the bleachers, the six-piece band played country favorites. The judges sang along in harmony.

Travis, heartbreaker handsome in his blue jacket and vest, waited next to Steve and Jasper Ridge at the head of the dirt aisle between the bleachers and the band. Cameras were everywhere. Anthony and the crew moved around the periphery, assessing all the angles, getting all the best shots.

And then came the moment she dreaded. Anthony signaled the band and they switched to the Wedding March. Brenna's stomach lurched. This was it. It was really going to happen.

Lori Luckly, wearing a headset and a pencil skirt with her cowboy boots, flung back the door to the van. She held out her hand to Roberta.

Roberta took it, stepping down, bringing her small bouquet of yellow flowers up, holding them before her in both hands. And then she was doing the wedding walk, all slow and stately, toward Trav, Steve and Jasper at the end of the dirt aisle. The soft hem of her yellow skirt fluttered in the slight wind.

Lori shot Brenna a bright smile. Numbly, Brenna touched the crown of daisies she'd chosen instead of a veil. Lori spoke softly into her headset and then held out her hand to help Brenna down. Careful of her long skirt, Brenna stepped to the ground. "Slow." Lori mouthed the word, handing Brenna a big bouquet of daisies and shiny white ribbons. "It's your moment," she said very softly. "Make it last."

Brenna's feet felt disconnected from the rest of her body. But somehow, with great effort, she got them to move. Going slowly was no problem. Every step was a monumental effort of will.

She focused on Trav's dear face and made herself move toward him.

Too soon, she was there, standing beside him as the Wedding March ended. Roberta took her bouquet and Trav took her hand. By then, she couldn't look at him. She swallowed convulsively as they both turned to face Jasper.

The man in black opened the gold-tooled Bible in his hands and cleared his throat. "Dearly beloved…" Jasper's lips moved, and Brenna stared at them blankly, not really hearing the words he said.

And then the wind came up. It made a high, keening sound. Like someone lost and crying. Brenna's skirts belled out, and her hair whipped wildly around her face.

And she…

Well, she just *couldn't*.

"Trav."

He squeezed her hand. "Bren? What…?" He tried to pull her closer. She dug in her boot heels and held her ground.

Jasper stopped his droning and cleared his throat again. "We got a problem?"

Oh, you bet we do. "I can't, Trav." It came out a ragged whisper as she pulled her hand free of his hold. "I'm so sorry. I just…well, I can't."

And then she picked up her big white skirts and sprinted off across the pasture toward the fence and the forest and the faraway mountains.

People shouted at her, but she didn't listen. And she didn't look back. Her heart breaking to bits inside her chest and her eyes blurry with tears, she just kept on running as fast as she could.

Chapter Twelve

Brenna was over the fence before Anthony and Roger started shouting. Anthony began barking orders to get a camera crew to follow her.

Trav knew he had to stop them. "Let her go!" he shouted as Brenna vanished from sight into the trees. The director, producer and crew ignored him.

At first.

But then he bellowed, "Let her go or I'm outta here, too. I will run and keep running. You won't catch up with either of us."

Steve said, "Me, too!"

And Roberta chimed in, "And me!"

And then the bleachers erupted. "Let her go!" shouted Fred Franklin.

"Leave her be!" hollered Wally.

"Leave her alone!" cried Leah Stone.

Even Summer joined in. "Back off, you damned idiots!"

Director, producer, wedding planner and every last soul on the crew—they all froze and stared, openmouthed, at the bleachers, where the cast of *The Great Roundup* shouted and stomped their feet, every one of them scowling, looking downright dangerous, like an unruly mob.

Trav grabbed Steve's arm. "Keep them here."

"You got it, man."

Pausing only to rip off his body mic and toss it to the ground, Travis took off across the pasture after his runaway bride.

She didn't go all that far.

A quarter of a mile or so into the trees, he found her sitting on a fallen log, looking like a sad and slightly lost redheaded angel in her white dress, with her crown of flowers drooping down her brow.

She shoved the flowers off her forehead and then, with a frustrated cry, she grabbed them and yanked them off her head altogether, tossing them angrily over her shoulder. "Trav." She blew a hank of hair out of her eyes. "I'm so sorry. I'm really, really –"

He put a finger to his lips. Then he mouthed, "Your mic."

She only moaned and hung her head, but at least she wasn't going anywhere. He dared to get closer. She didn't even look up when he sat down next to her, didn't object when he plucked the microphone from the front of her poufy dress and pulled it free of the transmitter. Rising, he tossed the mic off into the trees.

"Now." He sat down beside her again and captured her hand. At least she didn't pull away. He took heart from that. With a finger, he guided a swatch of hair behind her ear. "I think it's time you maybe talked to me."

She took a shaky breath. "Yeah," she said in a tiny voice. "Yeah, I guess it's time."

"Come here." He put both arms around her.

She sagged against him, resting her head on his shoulder with a surrendering sigh. "I just couldn't do it. I couldn't marry you."

He smoothed her tangled hair. "It's okay. I get it."

"Do you?" She sounded so lost, so completely alone.

He took her chin and made her look at him. "I mean it. It's okay. I'm with you. It's wrong. I see that. It's wrong, and we're not going through with it."

She sagged against him again. "I really thought I could, you know? I told myself, *Just focus on the win, just do what you have to do*. But I…I love you so much, Trav. I think I always have, through all the years, forever and ever, since you came to my rescue the first time when I was six years old. I can't marry you—not when I love you, and know that I have to divorce you. I just can't do that. I'm sorry. *That* is just too wrong."

Does every man have a moment when it all comes together?

When all at once his whole life makes total sense?

Travis did.

And that moment?

It was now.

He tipped up her chin again. The tears that shone in her eyes started falling. They ran down her cheeks.

She sniffed and swiped a hand under her reddened nose. "Ugh. I'm a mess."

"I have never seen anyone as beautiful as you, Bren. Never in my whole life."

She blew out her cheeks with a hard breath. "Yeah, right."

"It's true. And you…" His voice got snagged up. But he tried again and managed to ask the question in a low, rough growl. "You love me, Brenna? You really do?"

Tears dripping off her chin, she nodded.

"Good," he answered fervently. "Because, Bren, I love you, too."

She gasped. "Oh, Trav." She sniffed and then asked in a small voice, "You do? You really do?"

He brushed at her soft cheeks, wiping the wetness away. And suddenly the right words were there. He opened his mouth and let them out. "I love you, Brenna. Only you. I know I've fought it, my love for you. Fought it my whole life. At first you were too young for me. And then, well, somehow, I got stuck on a certain idea of myself, of being all about freedom, of not being the kind to settle down. But, Bren, if you love me, it all starts to make sense. Because why would I ever want to settle down with some other woman if you could be mine?"

She stared at him, her mouth a soft O. "Trav."

"What? Bren. Dear God. Please believe me."

She laughed. "Oh, Trav." And then she framed his face between her hands. "You'd better kiss me. Do it now."

He had absolutely no problem with that. Leaning in, he claimed her tearstained lips in a slow, ever-deepening kiss, a kiss that whispered of forever, a kiss that promised he would hold on tight to what they had. That he'd at last become the man she needed. The kind of man who would always be there to help her win every challenge she took on, to catch her if ever she needed a safe place to fall.

"Good," she said with a trembling smile when he finally lifted his head. "It's you and me, together."

"Together forever," he vowed.

And then she asked with a long sigh, "But what do we do now?"

"I know this much. I still want to marry you if you'll have me."

Her eyes gleamed so bright. "Oh, Trav. I will have you. I will never, ever let you go."

"Just not today. Because I want you to have the real thing in our little white church in Rust Creek Falls, with your sisters for your bridesmaids and our families filling every pew."

She widened those sea-blue eyes at him. "We are so gonna get sued. You know that, right?"

"I do—and yeah, it might get a little messy, breaking our contract."

She made a snorting sound. "A *little* messy?"

He kissed her red nose. "Think positive. Ryan Roarke is a hell of a lawyer, and he'll get us out of it somehow." She gazed up at him, her tear-filled eyes full of equal parts wonder and worry. He squeezed her shoulder. "So for today, we'll go back, face the others and tell them we are not saying our sacred vows on a reality show." He started to rise.

"Wait." She pulled him back down.

"What?"

"I just want to make this crystal clear. You are asking me to marry you—I mean, *really* marry you."

He took both her hands as he stood. And that time, she rose with him. "I am." He held her eyes. "Brenna

O'Reilly, I love you. Please say you'll marry me. Please tell me yes."

"Yes," she said, out loud and clear. "Yes, absolutely, I *will* marry you."

"That's what I wanted to hear." And he picked her up and whirled her around. She braced her hands on his shoulders and laughed, the sound echoing upward through the canopy of green over their heads. When he set her down, he grabbed her hand. "Come on now. Let's get it over with. We'll go tell Roger and the rest of them that we're not getting married on *The Great Roundup.*"

But she held him back. "This is real, right? I mean, this is really happening?"

"Real as it gets. Let's go."

But still she wouldn't budge. "Wait, Trav."

He gave in and turned to face her fully again. "What now?"

"Well, I'm thinking that if it's real, if we're getting married and staying that way—"

"Brenna, It's real and it's true and I can't wait to marry you."

"Well, then. You don't have to wait. Because I would love nothing so much as to get married to you right now, today, on *The Great Roundup,* where we finally found each other."

He frowned. "You know, when you put it that way, it doesn't sound half bad."

"Well, then. Let's do it."

He felt honor bound to remind her, "We would still have months ahead of us pretending that we're *not* married. How are we going to hold up through that?"

"I'm thinking I'm renting the apartment over the

beauty shop right away. And I'm also thinking you're going to be visiting your fiancée just about every night. People will be whispering how that wild Travis Dalton can't keep away from Brenna O'Reilly."

"That sounds amazing."

She nodded. "Yeah. I think so, too."

"And then, next year, if we win—"

"Oh, Trav, there's no doubt in my mind now. We're gonna win."

"*When* we win."

"That's better." She made a low, throaty sound of approval.

"I want to build a house for us on Dalton land."

"Yes. And I want to buy Bee out."

"Absolutely." He clasped her shoulders. "Look at me."

"Oh, Trav. I am."

"Are you sure?"

She didn't waver. "I've never been so sure about anything in my whole life."

That did it. He grabbed her close and kissed her again.

And then again. Because he loved her. Because forever stretched out in front of them and it looked full of promise now, bright as a new day. But whatever the future brought them, they would own it together.

From this day on.

"We need to agree on how to handle them," he whispered finally. "This, you and me, just now, it belongs to us. Nobody else. But we need a good story for the show."

"I have it. We tell the truth, just not *all* the truth." And she pulled him down to whisper in his ear.

* * *

"I see them!" someone shouted as Travis and Brenna emerged from the shelter of the trees. "They're coming!"

Brenna felt wonderful. She had it all now. She had Travis at her side and his promise to be there for the rest of their lives—a promise she believed in, a promise she returned.

He led her to the fence and helped her over it.

"You ready for this?" he asked as he set her down on solid ground.

"Oh, yes, I am."

Roger was furious, and Anthony seethed.

Brenna told them sweetly that she and Travis were ready now.

"Mic them up again!" Roger yelled. "Makeup! Wardrobe!"

A half an hour later, Brenna had a new body mic. Her makeup was flawless, and her hair was sleek and smooth, crowned with yellow daisies.

Roger called for OTFs. Brenna did hers sitting in a corner of the bleachers, her puffy skirts pulled up enough to show her purple boots, her wedding bouquet in her hand.

"I just got so emotional," she said with a long sigh. "I needed a minute to myself. You know, to deal with all the powerful, overwhelming feelings I was experiencing. And also, well, I did need a time-out with Travis, just the two of us."

"But you ran away," chided Roger. "How did you know he would follow you?"

"Of course, I couldn't be sure he would follow me

when I ran. But, oh, I did hope that he would. I needed to hear his words of love. I needed him to hold me in his strong arms."

"And how do you feel now, Brenna?"

"Now that I've gotten exactly what I needed, now that I've dealt with the enormity of this big step before me and spent a little time with my man, now I am definitely ready, willing and able to proudly and happily say 'I do.'"

By then, everyone was smiling, even Roger.

They all found their marks.

And Brenna O'Reilly married Travis Dalton in the middle of a pasture on *The Great Roundup*. They did it for real and forever—and for all the world to see.

Epilogue

That evening, after Brenna and Travis shared their first dance, Steve got down on his good knee and proposed to Roberta. Roberta burst into happy tears and cried out, "Yes!"

Three days later, Roberta was eliminated. Two days after that, Steve followed her.

The final challenge would pit Bren against Trav. They both loved that. No matter how it came out now, they'd won.

The next day, the bleachers went up again in the pasture where they'd said their wedding vows. The entire cast came out to watch.

The challenge: hay bale racing.

Trav knew he was beaten before the race began. Bren had taken more than one ribbon running barrels at the local rodeo. And she got that great little mare, Lady-girl, to ride.

But he got Applejack, a fine, fast gelding, his favorite of the mounts in the High Lonesome stables. And he gave the race his all, knowing Brenna would expect nothing less of him. He didn't mess up the cloverleaf pattern, and his time was damn good, too.

Hay bales or barrels, though, Bren still had what it took. She and Ladygirl looked like they were flying as they raced around those bales.

She beat his time by more than two seconds.

And that was how Brenna O'Reilly Dalton won a million dollars on *The Great Roundup*.

Or rather, that was how Brenna *and* Travis won. Together, they claimed both first and second prize and they would share their winnings equally, as they'd always agreed.

They had it all now and they both knew it. They had the money for a new start.

And most important, they had each other.

For the rest of their lives.

* * * * *

Look for the next installment of the new
Harlequin Special Edition continuity
MONTANA MAVERICKS:
THE GREAT FAMILY ROUNDUP

Filthy rich cowboy Autry Jones has watched with
amusement as two of his brothers have settled down
and become family men, but he's convinced it won't
happen to him. Until he meets pretty young widow
Marissa Fuller and her three little girls and falls for
all four of them...

Don't miss
MOMMY AND THE MAVERICK
by Meg Maxwell

On sale August 2017, wherever Harlequin books
and ebooks are sold.

Katrina Bailey's life is at a crossroads, so when arrogant—but sexy—Bowie Callahan asks for her help caring for his newly discovered half brother, she accepts, never expecting it to turn into something more...

Read on for a sneak peek at SERENITY HARBOR, the next book in the HAVEN POINT series by New York Times *bestselling author RaeAnne Thayne available July 2017!*

CHAPTER ONE

"THAT'S HIM AT your six o'clock, over by the tomatoes. Brown hair, blue eyes, ripped. Don't look. Isn't he *gorgeous*?"

Katrina Bailey barely restrained from rolling her eyes at her best friend. "How am I supposed to know that if you won't let me even sneak a peek at the man?" she asked Samantha Fremont.

Sam shrugged with another sidelong look in the man's direction. "Okay. You can look. Just make it subtle."

Mere months ago, all vital details about her best friend's latest crush might have been the most fascinating thing the two of them talked about all week. Right now, she found it tough to work up much interest in one more man in a long string of them, especially with everything else she had spinning in her life right now.

She wanted to ignore Sam's request and continue on with shopping for the things they needed to take to Wynona's shower—but friends didn't blow off their friends' obsessions. She loved Sam and had missed hanging out with her over the last nine months. It made her sad that their interests appeared to have diverged so dramatically, but it wouldn't hurt her to act like she cared about the cute newcomer to Haven Point.

Donning her best ninja spy skills- -honed from years

of doing this very thing, checking out hot guys without them noticing—she pretended to reach up to grab a can of peas off the shelf. She studied the label intently, all while shifting her gaze toward the other end of the aisle.

About ten feet away, she spotted two men. Considering she knew Darwin Twitchell well—and he was close to eighty years old and cranky as a badger with gout—the other guy had to be Bowie Callahan, the new director of research and development at the Caine Tech facility in town.

Years of habit couldn't be overcome by sheer force of will. That was the only reason her stomach muscles seemed to shiver and her toes curled against the leather of her sandals. Or so she told herself, anyway.

Okay. She got it. Sam was totally right. The man was indeed great-looking: tall, lean, tanned, with sculpted features and brown hair streaked with the sort of blond highlights that didn't come from a salon but from spending time outside.

Under other circumstances, she might have wanted to do more than look. In a different life, perhaps she would have made her way to his end of the aisle, pretended to fumble with an item on the shelf, then dropped it right at his feet so they could "meet" while they both reached to pick it up.

She used to be such an idiot.

The old Katrina might not have been able to look away from such a gorgeous male specimen. But when he aimed a ferocious scowl downward, she shifted her gaze to find him frowning at a boy who looked to be about five or six, trying his best to put a box of sugary cereal into their cart and growing visibly upset when

Bowie Callahan kept taking it out and putting it back on the shelf.

Katrina frowned. "You didn't say he had a kid. I thought you had a strict rule. No divorced dads."

"He doesn't have a kid!" Sam exclaimed.

"Then who's the little kid currently winding up for what looks like a world-class tantrum at his feet?"

Ignoring her own stricture about not staring, Sam whirled around. Her eyes widened with confusion. "I have no idea! I heard it straight from Eliza Caine that he's not married and doesn't have a family. He never said anything to me about a kid when I met him at a party at Snow Angel Cove or the other two times I've bumped into him around town this spring. I haven't seen him around for a few weeks. Maybe he has family visiting. Or maybe he's babysitting or something."

That was so patently ridiculous, Katrina had to bite her tongue. Really? Did Sam honestly believe the new director of research and development at Caine Tech would be offering babysitting services—in the middle of the day and on a Monday, no less?

She sincerely adored Samantha for a million different reasons, but sometimes her friend saw what she wanted to see.

This latest example of how their paths had diverged in recent months made her a little sad. Until a year ago, she and Sam had been— as her mom would say—two peas of the same pod. They shared the same taste in music, movies, clothes. They could spend hours poring over celebrity and fashion magazines, dishing about the latest gossip, shopping for bargains at thrift stores and yard sales.

And men. She didn't even want to think about how

many hours of her life she had wasted with Sam, talking about whichever guy they were most interested in that day.

Samantha had been her best friend since they found each other in junior high in that mysterious way like discovered like.

She still loved her dearly. Sam was kind and generous and funny, but Katrina's own priorities had shifted. After the events of the last year, Katrina was beginning to realize she barely resembled the somewhat shallow, flighty girl she had been before she grabbed her passport and hopped on a plane with Carter Ross.

That was a good thing, she supposed, but she felt a little pang of fear that while on the path to gaining a little maturity, she might end up losing her best friend.

"Babysitting. I suppose it's possible," she said in a noncommittal voice. If so, the guy was really lousy at it. The boy's face had reddened, and tears had started streaming down his features. By all appearances, he was approaching a meltdown, and Bowie Callahan's scowl had shifted to a look of helpless frustration.

"If you want, I can introduce you," Sam said, apparently oblivious to the drama.

Katrina purposely pushed their cart forward, in the opposite direction. "You know, it doesn't look like a good time. I'm sure I'll have a chance to meet him later. I'll be in Haven Point for a month. Between Wyn's wedding and Lake Haven Days, there should be plenty of time to socialize with our newest resident."

"Are you sure?" Sam asked, disappointment clouding her gaze.

"Yeah. Let's just finish shopping so I have time to go home and change before the shower."

Not that her mother's house really felt like home anymore. Yet another radical change in the last nine months.

"I guess you're right," Sam said, after another surreptitious look over Katrina's shoulder. "We waited too long, anyway. Looks like he's moved to another aisle."

They found the items they needed and moved to the next aisle as well, but didn't bump into Bowie again. Maybe he had taken the boy, whoever he was, out of the store so he could cope with his meltdown in private.

They were nearly finished shopping when Sam's phone rang with the ominous tone she used to identify her mother.

She pulled the device out of her purse and glared at it. "I wish I dared to ignore her, but if I do, I'll hear about it for a week."

That was nothing, she thought. If Katrina ignored *her* mother's calls while she was in town for Wyn's wedding, Charlene would probably mount a search and rescue, which was kind of funny when she thought about it. Charlene hadn't been nearly as smothering when Kat had been living halfway around the world in primitive conditions for the last nine months. But if she dared show up late for dinner, sheer panic ensued.

"I'm at the grocery store with Kat," Samantha said, a crackly layer of irritation in her voice. "I texted you that's where I would be."

Her mother responded something Katrina couldn't hear, which made Sam roll her eyes. To others, Linda Fremont could be demanding and cranky, quick to criticize. Oddly, she had always treated Katrina with tolerance and even a measure of kindness.

"Do you absolutely need it tonight?" Samantha

asked, pausing a moment to listen to her mother's answer with obvious impatience written all over her features. "Fine. Yes. I can run over. I only wish you had mentioned this earlier, when I was just hanging around for three hours doing nothing, waiting for someone to show up at the shop. I'll grab it."

She shut off her phone and shoved it back into her little dangly Coach purse that she'd bought for a steal at the Salvation Army in Boise. "I need to stop in next door at the drugstore to pick up one of my mom's prescriptions. Sorry. I know we're in a rush."

"No problem. I'll finish the shopping and check out, then we can meet each other at your car when we're done."

"Hey, I just had a great idea," Sam exclaimed. "After the shower tonight, we should totally head up to Shelter Springs and grab a drink at the Painted Moose!"

Katrina tried not to groan. The last thing she wanted to do amid her lingering jet lag was visit the local bar scene, listening to the same songs, flirting with the same losers, trying to laugh at their same old, tired jokes.

"Let's play it by ear. We might be having so much fun at the shower that we won't want to leave. Plus it's Monday night, and I doubt there will be much going on at the PM."

She didn't have the heart to tell Sam she wasn't the same girl who loved nothing more than dancing with a bunch of half-drunk cowboys—or that she had a feeling she would never be that girl again. Priorities had a way of shifting when a person wasn't looking.

Sam stuck her bottom lip out in an exaggerated pout.

"Don't be such a party pooper! We've only got a month together, and I've missed you *so much*!"

Great. Like she needed more guilt in her life.

"Let's play it by ear. Go grab your mom's prescription, I'll check out and we'll head over to Julia's place. We can figure out our after-party plans, well, after the party."

She could tell by Sam's pout that she would have a hard time escaping a late night with her. Maybe she could talk her into just hanging out by the lakeshore and talking.

"Okay. I guess we'd better hurry if we want to have time to make our salad."

Sam hurried toward the front doors, and Katrina turned back to her list. Only the items from the vegetable aisle, then she would be done. She headed in that direction and spotted a flustered Bowie Callahan trying to keep the boy with him from eating grapes from the display.

"Stop it, Milo. I told you, you can eat as many as you want *after* we buy them."

This only seemed to make the boy more frustrated. She could see by his behavior and his repetitive mannerisms that he quite possibly had some sort of developmental issues. Autism, she would guess at a glance—though that could be a gross generalization, and she was not an expert, anyway.

Whatever the case, Callahan seemed wholly unprepared to deal with it. He hadn't taken the boy out of the store, obviously, to give him a break from the overstimulation. In fact, things seemed to have progressed from bad to worse.

Milo—cute name —reached for another grape despite the warning, and Bowie grabbed his hand and sternly looked down into his face. "I said, stop it. We'll have grapes after we pay for them."

The boy didn't like that. He wrenched his hand away and threw himself to the ground. "No! No! No!" he chanted.

"That's enough," Bowie Callahan snapped, loudly enough that other shoppers turned around to stare, which made the man flush.

She could see Milo was gearing up for a nuclear meltdown—and while she reminded herself it was none of her business, she couldn't escape a certain sense of professional obligation to step in.

She wanted to ignore it, to turn into the next aisle, finish her shopping and escape the store as quickly as she could. She could come up with a dozen excuses about why that was the best course of action. Samantha would be waiting for her. She didn't know the man or his frustrated kid. She had plenty of troubles of her own to worry about.

None of that held much weight when compared with the sight of a child, who clearly had some special needs, in great distress—and an adult who just as clearly didn't know what to do in the situation.

She felt an unexpected pang of sympathy for Bowie Callahan, probably because her mother had told her so many stories about how mortified Charlene would be when Katrina would have a seizure in a public place. All the staring, the pointing, the whispers.

The boy continued to chant, "No," and began smacking his palm against his forehead in rhythm with each exclamation. A couple of older women she didn't know—tourists, probably—looked askance at the boy, and one muttered something to the other about how some children needed a swat on the behind.

She wanted to tell the old biddies to mind their own business but held her tongue, since she was about to ignore her own advice.

After another minute passed, when Bowie Callahan did nothing but gaze down at the boy with helpless frustration, Katrina knew she had to act. What other choice did she have? She pushed her cart closer. The man briefly met her gaze with a wariness that she chose to ignore. Instead, she plopped onto the ground next to the distressed boy.

In her experience with children of all ages and abilities, they reacted better to someone willing to lower to their level. She wasn't sure if he even noticed she was there, since he didn't stop chanting or smacking his palm against his head.

"Hi there." She spoke in a calm, conversational tone, as if she was chatting with one of her friends at Wynona's shower later in the evening. "What's your name?"

Milo— whose name she knew perfectly well from hearing Bowie use it —barely took a breath. "No! No! No! No!"

"Mine is Katrina," she went on. "Some people call me Kat. You know. Kitty-cat. Meow. Meow."

His voice hitched a little, and he lowered his hand but continued chanting, though he didn't sound quite as distressed. "No. No. No."

"Let me guess," she said. "Is your name Batman?"

He frowned. "No. No. No."

"Is it… Anakin Skywalker?"

She picked the name, assuming by his Star Wars T-shirt it would be familiar to him. He shook his head. "No."

"What about Harry Potter?"

This time, he looked intrigued at the question, or perhaps at her stupidity. He shook his head.

"How about Milo?"

Big blue eyes widened with shock. "No," he said, though his tone gave the word the opposite meaning.

"Milo. Hi there. I like your name. I've never met anybody named Milo. Do you know anybody else named Kat?"

He shook his head.

"Neither do I," she admitted. "But I have a cat. Her name is Marshmallow, because she's all white. Do you like marshmallows? The kind you eat, I mean."

He nodded and she smiled. "I do, too. Especially in hot cocoa."

He pantomimed petting a cat and pointed at her.

"You'd like to pet her? She would like that. She lives with my mom now and loves to have anyone pay attention to her. Do you have a cat or a dog, Milo?"

The boy's forehead furrowed, and he shook his head, glaring up at the man beside him, who looked stonily down at both of them.

Apparently that was a touchy subject.

Did the boy talk? She had heard him say only "no" so far. It wasn't uncommon for children on the autism spectrum and with other developmental delays to have much better receptive language skills than expressive skill, and he obviously understood and could get his response across fairly well without words.

"I see lots of delicious things in your cart—including cherries. Those are my favorite. Yum. I must have missed those. Where did you find them?"

He pointed to another area of the produce section,

where a gorgeous display of cherries gleamed under the fluorescent lights.

She pretended she didn't see them. Though the boy's tantrum had been averted for now, she didn't think it would hurt anything if she distracted him a little longer. "Do you think you could show me?"

It was a technique she frequently employed with her students who might be struggling, whether that was socially, emotionally or academically. She found that if she enlisted their help—either to assist her or to help out another student—they could often be distracted enough that they forgot whatever had upset them.

Milo craned his neck to look up at Bowie Callahan for permission. The man looked down at both of them, a baffled look on his features, but after a moment he shrugged and reached a hand down to help her off the floor.

She didn't need assistance, but it would probably seem rude to ignore him. She placed her hand in his and found it warm and solid and much more calloused than a computer nerd should have. She tried not to pay attention to the little shock of electricity between them or the tug at her nerves.

"Thanks," she mumbled, looking quickly away as she followed the boy, who, she was happy to notice, seemed to have completely forgotten his frustration.

Don't miss SERENITY HARBOR
by RaeAnne Thayne
available wherever HQN books and ebooks are sold!

SPECIAL EXCERPT FROM

H HARLEQUIN®

SPECIAL EDITION

Billionaire businessman Autry Jones swore off single mothers—until he meets widowed mom of three Marissa Jones just weeks before he's supposed to leave for a job in Paris...

Read on for a sneak preview of
MOMMY AND THE MAVERICK
by **Meg Maxwell**, *the second book in the*
MONTANA MAVERICKS: THE GREAT FAMILY
ROUNDUP continuity.

"Right. We shook on being friends. But..." She paused and dropped down onto the love seat across from the fireplace.

"But things feel more than friendly between us," he finished for her. "There was that kiss, for one. And the fact that every time I see you I want to kiss you again."

"Ditto. See the problem?"

He smiled and sat down beside her. "Marissa, why did you come here? To tell me that doing the competition with Abby is a bad idea? That she's going to get too attached to me?"

"Yup."

"Except you didn't say that."

"Because I don't want to take it from her. I want her to be excited about the competition. To not lose out on something when she's been dealt a hard blow in life so young. But yeah, I am worried she's going to get too attached. All three girls. But especially Abby."

"Abby knows I'm leaving for Paris at the end of August. That's a given. Goodbye is already in the air, Marissa. We're not fooling anyone."

"Why do I keep fighting it, then?" she asked. "Why do I have to keep reminding myself that feeling the way I do about you is only going to—"

"Make you feel like crap when I go? I know. I've had that same talk with myself fifty times. I wasn't expecting to meet you, Marissa. Or want you so damned bad every time I see you."

It wasn't just about sex, but he wasn't putting that out there. If she kept it to sexual attraction, surface stuff, maybe he'd believe it. Then he could enjoy his time with Marissa and go in a couple weeks without much strain in his chest.

"So what do we do?" she asked. "Give in to this or be smart and stay nice and platonic?"

He reached for her hand. "I don't know."

"Your hair's still damp," she said. "I can smell your shampoo. And your soap."

He leaned closer and kissed her, his hands slipping around her shoulders, down her back, drawing her to him. He felt her stiffen for a second and then relax. "I don't want to just be friends, Marissa. I want you."

She kissed him back, her hands in his hair, and he could feel her breasts against his chest. He sucked in a breath, overwhelmed by desire, by need. "You're sure?" he asked, pulling back a bit to look at her, directly into her beautiful dark brown eyes.

"No, I'm not sure," she whispered. "I just know that I want you, too."

Don't miss
MOMMY AND THE MAVERICK by Meg Maxwell,
available August 2017 wherever
Harlequin® Special Edition books and ebooks are sold.

www.Harlequin.com